Beautifully Broken
Cassandra Moll

Cover design: Caravelle Creates

First edition: November 2024

ISBN: 9798991826006 (paperback)

For my village.
You know who you are.

"Tough times never last, but tough people do."
-Robert Schuller

"Tough times never last, but tough people do."
-Robert Schuller

Beautifully Broken

Prologue
Jamison – 18 Years Earlier

I'm crouching down as low as I can, pulling my knees close to my belly to stay wedged between two stalks. We're hiding in the cornfield like minnows under rocks, trying not to get eaten by the large-mouth bass. Mommy says we're on an adventure like Huck Finn, and we have to be sneaky just like him. Something is digging into my bare foot, but I'm trying my best to stay still because Mommy says we can't be seen and we can't be heard.

"Just a little longer, Jamison," she whispers.

Mommy always calls me Jamison. Not Jay like everyone else. She says that Jamison is a strong name, and I'm a strong boy, and I shouldn't make any part of myself smaller for someone else. It's the name she uses when she calls me for dinner and when she tells me I better not be acting out in school. It's also the one she used earlier running from the house.

"Come, Jamison. Now. We're going on an adventure. Start running, baby, and don't look back."

We run through the cornfield that sits behind our house. I don't know who owns it, but it must belong to someone because every year corn shows up and every year they chop it down. On the other side of the field, I hear yelling. It sounds like the slur of Bill's words I've heard so often in the last month. I look at Mommy, and she puts her first finger to her lips and reaches around the stalk between us to squeeze my hand. He's mad. I can tell by the way Mommy's eyes dart around like the rolly-pollies do when I pick up the big rocks in the backyard. Her forehead is wrinkled and she's pretending to smile. Sweat forms on the edge of her face where her skin starts and her red hair ends.

Mommy's hand is sweaty and my foot is really starting to hurt. It's only now that I realize we aren't having an adventure. Adventures are fun and exciting. This is scary and strange. No, this isn't an adventure. We are hiding.

We are hiding from Bill and his sour breath, his bruised fists, and his worn belt. We are playing Huck Finn but not the part where he rides the river and smokes cigars and pretends. We are playing the part where he is a prisoner and alone and he runs from his daddy who is a drunk and a monster.
Bill is mad. He's drunk and mad, and he's coming.
He's the bass.
And we are the minnows.

1

Jamison

I was six the first time I remember running into a cornfield to hide from my mom's piece of shit boyfriend. It wasn't the first time I remember hiding though. In closets, under the porch, behind the thorn bushes that tore up my exposed skin — pretty much any spot a normal kid would choose for hide and seek is what I used as a refuge from drunk and high wife-beaters. It's one of the many reasons that I black out my younger days as much as possible.

I guess at twenty-four, some would say I'm still in the prime of my so-called youth, but I haven't felt young for as long as I can remember. And it's remembering that's the problem. Like now, when the early June heat takes me back to that day in the field. Before now, I hadn't thought about that day for a while.

I stand outside of Monroe's Motors, taking my second official 10-minute break. I guess it's my "smoke break," but when a Newport sits between my fingers more times than not, it's not technically needed. Either way, I'm entitled to it so you bet your ass I'm taking it, especially when I've worked six of the last seven days.

I've been a mechanic officially for eight years now, having started with small jobs in the shop right at sixteen, but I've been messing with cars for as long as I can remember. My fingers seem permanently stained from engine oil and my back constantly aches from hanging in cars. Already today I've had four cups of black coffee just to keep me coherent from my usual lack of sleep and this lingering dull headache is a physical reminder of my mental agony. *What a fucking winner.*

"Jay, let's go!"

My boss interrupts my self-loathing long enough for me to realize my cigarette is burned to the filter and my ten-minute break is more than over. I flick the ash and crush the butt against the wall before tossing it into the standing ashtray, then turn to walk back to the front bay doors.

Inside, I see her. The hottest thing I've seen in a long time. No, scratch that. Ever. Smooth curves, well-built, polished, and clean. Damn, I would kill to get under that hood.

"Hey, Jay! Close your mouth, man!" my friend, coworker, and long-time pain in my ass Sean says, clapping me on the back. He points his index finger to my chin so close I ought to snap it off.

"You got a little drool right...there."

He grazes my chin with his fingertip, and I smack his hand away with the back of mine. Sean just doesn't get it. He doesn't see what I see when I look at the beauty that sits in front of me. With perfect timing, Zeke approaches us and tells me what I already know.

"302-Powered, 1974 Ford Maverick Grabber. Pretty sweet, huh?"

Sweet was not what I was thinking. This car is sexy as hell.

"The owner's a long-time customer of mine. Just dropped it off. He wants us to take a look at it and make sure everything is in order. Says he's looking to sell it and doesn't want any potential buyers trying to lower the price on some made-up bullshit."

"Sell it?" I say loudly, more aggravated than I mean to.

"Yep," Zeke answers, ignoring my tone. "His dad passed away and left it to him. He says it's just not his thing. Takes up too much room and isn't worth the upkeep."

I scoff under my breath. See, this is what's wrong with people. They get something good, something special, something that maybe requires some space, some care, and decency...some love, and they throw it away because they don't feel like dealing with it. This is why I love cars. If you take care of them, the older they get, the more valuable they are. Cars mean more as long as you protect them, love them, and keep them clean and fed with the best fluids and nutrients.

Kind of like kids.

Or so I'm told.

The phone rings and snaps me out of my silent rant. Zeke turns towards it, seemingly indifferent to me and my internal monologue.

"So, anyway," he calls from over his shoulder to us, Sean looking at me with a wrinkled brow. "You two take a good look and let me know what you come up with."

Sean just stares at me now with a half-smile on his face, shaking his head.

"Man, you should see someone about that zoning-out thing you do. You daydream more than a damn teenage girl." He walks to circle the car, but not before smirking and shooting me a wink. Smartass.

"Shut the hell up and lift the car," I hiss back, returning his wink with my middle finger.

Daydreams — yeah, right.

More like nightmares.

Just all of the time.

2

Claire

I pull out onto the main street of Maple Grove, making sure to check all of my mirrors first, if only for effect. I never drive my dad anywhere. He's critical of how I brush my teeth, let alone how I operate a vehicle, so, when he asked me to pick him up at Monroe's, I wasn't necessarily excited. Regardless, I love my dad and the distance between the garage and his house is barely a mile, so here I am.

I didn't realize Dad was just going to sell Grandpa's latest hot rod after he died. Grandpa probably didn't either for that matter or he might not have left it to him in his will, but I guess it's a little late for that. Dad never cared about cars, and he constantly fought with Grandpa, so the fact that it is worth a decent penny, is just a bonus I think. Still, this is just like him — practical and decisive.

"That thing is just going to sit around and collect dust, Claire," Dad says, turning to me. I didn't ask, but I think maybe he's saying it more for himself. "Not to mention the space it takes up in that darn garage your mother is always complaining about."

It's true. Mom complains about how messy and unorganized the garage is every time the seasons change or a new holiday approaches and she ventures into it looking for her decorations.

"Besides," he continues, this time turning his head and staring out the passenger window. "Your Grandpa spent so much time working on these cars — cleaning them, waxing them, messing around in their already pristine engines. Just not sure I care to constantly look at the thing that kept him from ever spending time with your grandmother and me."

I have heard stories about Dad's childhood and how unloved and ignored he seemed to feel. It is, I assume, the reason he is so critical of me. Having a parent who didn't seem to notice *anything*, evidently turns you into a parent who notices *everything*.

"I get it, Dad," I say boldly so he doesn't feel the need to further explain. And I do get it. If this is what keeps him from the constant reminder that even a two-door metal frame got more attention than him growing up, who am I to tell him to keep it?

Dad exhales loudly at my understanding but seems somewhat sad now, his right temple resting gently on the passenger window. His eyes start to glaze over staring at the passing cars, but we're barely through the next light when he lifts his head.

"Speed limit is thirty-five, Claire Bear."

And he's back. I playfully roll my eyes, looking at my speedometer that reads thirty-nine. Dad's not a square, but he is definitely not one for risk.

"Oh is it?" I joke back, pushing my foot to the gas just ever-so-slightly so that the speed now reads forty-three. Dad nudges my arm light-heartedly, but his face tells me he is not amused. He always means well. Half of the time I don't think he even realizes he's finding fault in little things. It's why I don't hold it against him, but it's also why I think I've been programmed to stress over every little thing myself.

"I'm going to need you to come over tomorrow around three," he declares as we pull into the driveway.

"Is that so? And what makes you think I don't have plans?"

"You do," he says matter-of-factly. "It's to be here at three." He unhooks his seatbelt, kisses my cheek, and exits the car ending the conversation. Ah, the joys of living right down the street from my parent's house.

I got my first teaching job as an English teacher right out of college at Jefferson Middle School just a few blocks from my childhood home. When they found out, my parents were insistent that I come back home and save money.

"It's silly to waste your hard-earned money on your own place when you'd practically live alone here anyway."

It's true that they are around even less than I am. My dad works long hours in finance and is usually either at his main office downtown or tucked away in his office at home, and Mom — her calendar is fuller than mine, mostly with the church, always helping with this or volunteering with that. More often than not she's grabbing lunch or doing a charcuterie class with someone I don't even know.

Despite all of this, I love my parents and my plan was to keep it that way. I just had a feeling that if I moved back in with them, a war may just erupt right under their roof. So instead, I got an apartment just down the road that I could afford on my teaching salary. I'm far enough away to feel like an actual grown-up not living at home with Mommy and Daddy, but close enough that I'm still very susceptible to favors. Especially when school's out.

A slight panic starts to build as I consider how my situation may change now with everything going on. *Will I have to move back home?* I shake the imposing thought from my head. It's just my normal summer break. I will deal with everything else soon enough.

I sigh to myself, pushing the button to lower the window. Dad is halfway up the walk when I stick my head out. "And why do I need to be here at three again?"

"Because Zeke is driving the Maverick back, and I need you to let him into the garage."

Clasping my hands together in prayer, I push the upper half of my body out of the window. In mock desperation, I plead "Pretty please, Claire? My favorite daughter!"

"You're my only daughter, Bear!" Dad calls as he pushes open the front door. "And I love ya!"

"Yeah yeah, love you too, Dad," I mumble, pulling my body back inside.

In reality, I don't have plans, just a tutoring session in the morning, but it'd be nice to at least be *asked* to come by. Regardless, I guess I have plans now — to open the garage door for our local mechanic. Sounds thrilling. And simple enough.

3

Jamison

16 Years Earlier

I hear the front door open and then quickly slam shut. There's yelling. Mommy cries out and something crashes to the floor. The lamp maybe? They're home.

I open my bedroom door just enough to fit three fingers between it and the frame. I know if I do it any further, the hinges will squeak and they'll hear me. I don't want them to hear me. I wish I couldn't hear them.

Mommy is on the couch, pushed so far into the corner that it looks like she's trying to melt into it. Her head is turned away from me and both of her hands are up, palms out, protecting herself. Sam, Mommy's new friend, hovers over her. His fists are clenched and his hair hangs over one eye that's squinting like he's trying hard to concentrate. He throws a punch towards Mommy's face. She shrieks and scrunches up as small as she can. I wince at the sounds — both of Mommy's cries and the contact that Sam's fist makes with the side of her head.

He tries to stand upright but stumbles back just a step. It's then that Mommy drops her hands just enough to turn towards my door. She can see I'm watching, and I can see the trickle of red that falls down the side of her face. Should I help her? This is the part that I don't understand. I want to run out, throw myself at him, and use my fist like Jackson taught me before he left. But Mommy always tells me not to cause trouble.

"You stay where you are, Jamison, you hear me? If there are ever any problems, you leave it to the grown-ups. You hide where you are and you don't come out until I come and get you, understand?"

I tell Mommy I do, but I really don't. I know I'm only eight, but why can't I at least try to help?

I push the door open just another inch or two, even though I know that hinge is gonna squeak. Maybe he'll stop if he knows I'm watching. The other ones didn't, but maybe he'll be different.

Sam's head snaps to the door. He chuffs, looking at Mommy and then back to me. He takes a step toward the couch and holds Mommy's chin with his first two fingers. He raises an eyebrow and smirks before looking at me.

"That's a cute kid you got, you know?" He turns back to Mommy and she flashes a tiny smile, but I know her enough to understand she's anything but happy.

He releases her chin and as quick as I blink, he slaps the back of his hand over Mommy's tear-stained face.

"He'll be next if I ever catch you lookin' at another man like you did tonight," he says before spitting in my direction. He sways back and forth, then points to Mommy so close he can probably feel her heavy breath. "And you, you good-for-nothing piece of shit — you can watch."

I wake up to the sound of my alarm, covered in a damp sweat, no different than any other morning. I rarely sleep and when I do, this is how I'm rewarded. Nightmares from my past that still haunt me in the present.

I reach for my nightstand, past my short stack of books, and turn off the voice on the FM radio announcing that "Maple Grove is getting hit with an early heat wave and a sweltering ninety-four degrees by noon." Awesome. I grab my cigarettes, still open from my bedtime smoke last night, and realize there are only two left. That should be enough to get me through until I stop on my way to work. Thirty-two minutes until my shift. I think I can manage.

I know cigarettes are *so out*. At least that's what Sean keeps reminding me. He says I need to "get with this decade" and switch to a vape. Even refuses to ride anywhere with me unless we take his car because apparently, mine smells like an old strip club.

"And not like the cool classy ones either where you still have to leave your phone at the door," he says, as if classy was a word usually used to describe these places. *"You know what I mean?"*

I don't know what he means because I would never be caught in any strip club, let alone one of *that* variety, but I get his point. It's just that when you've been smoking half a pack a day for half of your life, it doesn't matter what's in and what's "out." I'm not doing it to be cool so much as to not tear someone's head off every time they look at me wrong. I take one last drag before I force myself to get up and shower. I stride the whole four feet it takes to get to the bathroom, one perk of living in an actual closet, shed my boxer briefs, and take the most mediocre, lukewarm shower known to man.

My apartment, if you can call it that, is in the back of a pizza shop. Not on top. Not behind. Nope, literally in the back of a pizza shop. My best friend opened Enzo's a few years back and had the extra storage closet turned into an "apartment" by adding a bed, a toilet, and a makeshift kitchenette — basically a glorified counter with a sink, microwave, and George Foreman grill. It's small and constantly smells like oil from the fryer, but he offered it to me with no deposit needed. There's a door right down the hall that leads to the back parking lot, so I don't have to cut through the kitchen to come and go, and most importantly, it's cheap. Like highway robbery cheap compared to the average rent of places around here. Plus, it was the perfect solution at the time.

I dry off and throw on the same faded jeans from yesterday and a semi-clean Monroe's t-shirt. I lace up my boots with just enough time to fill a chipped travel mug with coffee before heading out the door. The second I step outside I'm blasted with heat like the Devil's ass. Tucking my coffee in the crook of my arm, I reach for my cigarettes and light my last one as I walk across the gravel lot behind Enzo's. I open and shut the door to my old 1991 Chevy Shitbox and crank the key, giving it the time it needs to clammer to life.

As I wait, my mind drifts back to my dream from last night. I revisit my past while I sleep, more often than I don't. It's crazy how something that happened so long ago can still live in your memory in such vivid detail. In my conscious hours, I tuck that shit as far back as I can, fully aware that by doing that, I have greatly contributed to my fucked-up-ness. I'm sure I should see a therapist or three, but for what? So they can tell me that I didn't deserve to watch my mother get beaten? That I was too young to handle the emotional and physical abuse I endured? Doesn't take a shrink to tell me what I already know. That night when I was eight was one of a million just like it. It's the reason I learned to fight. The reason I keep my walls high and my head low. The reason I don't let anyone in.

The engine hums to life pulling me back to the present. I roll down the window and turn the radio dial to the first station that lands on music rather than traffic or weather. The rhythmic guitar and subtle percussion of the Red Hot Chili Peppers pour from the speakers as the lead singer describes never again wanting to feel like he did when he was sad and alone.

Unfuckingbelievable. I let out one long breath, drag my hand down my face, and put the truck in drive as I head to work for another day in goddamn paradise.

4

Claire

Summers off are always weird. It's like fantasy and reality coexist. Like you're on vacation where days blur together, but you're also living your real life. It's like you want to feel like possibilities are endless and responsibilities are nonexistent, but really, it's your boredom that's endless and your paychecks nonexistent.

Despite the schedule change, I try to keep somewhat of an outline of my routine. Wake up at a decent hour, run, cross some things off my to-do list, and write at least one thing. I just do best when I keep busy. I've also been tutoring a few times each week since the spring to make some extra cash. Besides that, I try to help my parents as much as possible — hence my sitting outside on their front step, sweating more than I'd like to admit, at 3:20 in the afternoon.

Dad said 3 pm and Dad is always precise. So, I've been out here for twenty minutes baking in a tank top and jean shorts. Could I have used my key and gone inside to sit in the air-conditioning? Sure. But by the time I reined in my most recent panic regarding the end of the summer, the schvitzing was past the point of no return.

I'm pulling my sweat-soaked hair into a loose top knot when the car finally turns onto the street. I hear it before I see it, the revving of the engine so out of place in this quiet neighborhood. As the orange muscle car approaches the driveway I'm reminded of how nice it is. Knowing absolutely zero about cars, I have no idea what the big deal is with how it's built or the custom paint, but even a motor moron like me can see the thing is stunning. The sunlight dances off the windshield as it turns into the open spot next to my white Nissan, making it look impressively average in comparison.

I stand, pulling down my shorts that have now been swallowed by my slick thighs, and stroll over to the driver's side of the car. The way the sun is positioned on the window I can't quite see inside but I do catch a glimpse of my reflection. Despite my lack of makeup, my cheeks are pink, thanks to the heat, and I did manage to swipe just a covering of mascara to my already dark lashes. Being home alone most of the day, I'll take any excuse to at least do *something* with my appearance.

The owner of Monroe's has done the inspections and oil changes on all of our cars for as long as I can remember. He is right around my dad's age, and unfortunately already balding. His height is (very) slightly below average and his beer belly is (very) slightly above average, but he's a nice enough guy. Nice enough that I respect him more than just rolling out of bed, but these last twenty minutes have pretty much shot any effort right to Hell.

The window lowers slowly and...wait a second...that's not Zeke. Staring back at me is like a blonde, grease monkey version of Adam Levine, but with more muscle. My eyes scan him quickly, following the length of his tattooed biceps down to his grip on the steering wheel, and judging by the vein in his forearm alone, yep, definitely more muscle. I mean, he's not even Zeke-adjacent. I catch myself staring just a second too late when the guy behind the wheel clears his throat.

"Do you mind?" His voice is low and dull. He's looking at me with a blank expression and hazel eyes that are quite possibly piercing my soul as we speak.

I close my still-parted lips. "Excuse me?"

A blank expression stares back at me. Mystery Man blinks twice and moves his hand to the door handle. Good Lord those eyes.

Nodding out the window he clarifies, "Do you mind?"

"Oh!" I all but jump out of the way of the door. "Of course, sorry about that."

Unlike Zeke, this guy is right around my age and although his light hair is clipped short, almost military style, he is absolutely not balding. He stands at much more of an (above) average height and has much less (zero) beer belly. However, the stern face he wears mixed with the curt, "It's all good," he throws my way, tells me that, unlike Zeke, he is not necessarily a nice enough guy.

"I was expecting someone else," I clarify as I watch his left bicep flex beneath his shirt sleeve as he shuts the car door. Fully extended, I see this arm's tattoos — a tiger, a rose with thorns, and...is that a naked lady?

The distraction causes me to ramble on about my dad, the car, Zeke, and the time, and all too late I realize that I'm spiraling. So, in my attempt to reverse this unfortunate moment I finish off my monologue with a way too chippy, "But here you are!" *Good one Claire.*

Seemingly unbothered by my attempt at pleasantry, Mr. Personality shoves both hands in his pockets and simply echoes, "Here I am."

I'm starting to get the feeling this guy is incapable of stringing more than three words together when he adds, "Zeke got tied up with something so he asked me to come instead." I offer an understanding nod, shocked by his abundance of words.

He pulls his right hand from his pocket, offering me the keys. I take note of the tattoos that this arm reveals as it is stretched towards me. A bird spans the inside of his forearm, the silhouette of a person on the outside, and just above that, some sort of angel that is partially covered by his sleeve. Admittedly, he might have had his wrist dangling there longer than I realize because he lets out a slight huff and jingles the keys.

"Actually..." I pause hoping he'll fill the space with his name.

"Jay."

Hmm, simple. Shocker.

"Actually Jay, do you mind pulling it into the garage for me? I have no idea what I am doing with that thing and my dad would kill me if I scratched it."

His eyes glint with the slightest sparkle of — Is that joy? — but then it quickly fades.

"Not a problem." And, we're back to the three-word thing.

Turning back to the car, I can't help but notice how his shirt strains to accommodate his back muscles. I press the code for the garage into the keypad and watch the door smoothly roll open. Jay turns the engine, revving it just slightly, before parking it safely inside. He opens the door, but not before grabbing a small teal box from the passenger seat. Is that a pack of cigarettes? Do people still smoke those? And then it's like deja vu as he once again waves his wrist at me, offering me the keys. This time I take them, noticing the grease stains hiding under his fingernails.

"Thank you. I know my dad appreciates this."

"It's an awesome car. Can't believe he wants to sell it in the first place."

"Wow." I say it out loud by accident, but I am just shocked at the length of that sentence. "I mean, yeah, it's a long story. It was my grandfather's." I play with the key ring waiting for him to decide what's next.

He raises his head just slightly in understanding, his face suddenly breaking from indifference to what seems slightly sad.

"Alright well, I'm going to take off..." This time it's him who offers a pause for *my* name.

"Claire."

"Claire," Jay repeats and the way my name suddenly sounds so foreign to me catches me off guard — in a good way.

"Take care." He shoves his hands back into his pockets and turns towards the street. It's only when he's halfway down the driveway that I realize that he's leaving and for some strange, masochistic reason, I don't want him to. This man has said a total of twenty words to me and none of them have been particularly nice, yet I don't want him to go.
He also has no ride.

"Jay!" I call out suddenly both sounding and feeling desperate. "Do you want a ride? Back to Monroe's I mean?" I stand there like an eager puppy waiting for a treat.

"Nah, it's cool." Turning back to look at me he shakes his head and points his thumb over his shoulder. "It's not far. I'll walk."

"Are you sure? I seriously don't mind."

He nods, "I'm sure," then turns and continues leaving. He gets only a few more feet before I call after him again.

"Come on, don't be silly. My mom would damn me to Hell if I didn't drive you back. Please? For the sake of my soul?" Okay, seriously, now I'm begging.

I guess the third time's the charm because, after a two-second pause that felt like an eternity, he starts walking towards my SUV. I run to the hook inside the garage that holds my parents' keys and drop the Maverick's. Reaching into my pocket, I offer him a satisfied smile before clicking the button on my own keys to unlock the doors. I get in first, then him, and when he reaches for his seatbelt, his shirt rises just enough to reveal the slightest sliver of the skin above his jeans. All of a sudden the heat outside is nothing compared to what I feel in here. Completely unaware of the effect he has on me, he clicks his buckle down and looks at me waiting for me to do the same. Again, with the eyes-piercing-my-soul thing!

I repeat the gesture, start the car, and crank the A.C. up to full blast. *You're being ridiculous*, I think to myself.

Besides, it's one mile.

How bad could it be?

5

Jamison

That was pretty bad. Claire drove me the four minutes it took to get from her dad's house to Monroe's and not a single word was spoken. The silence didn't bother me much — I'm used to living with only my thoughts — but she was clearly uncomfortable. I, however, was uncomfortable for a different reason. Who is this girl? And why when I saw her sitting on that step was I flushed with such an unfamiliar feeling?

I could see her as I approached her house and the way she so casually pulled her long, loose waves on top of her head hypnotized me. Not to mention the way her shorts bunched when she stood, revealing her tan, toned thighs.

When she came to the window I could tell she was looking at her reflection. What she didn't realize was that while she was looking at herself, I was looking at her too. She was stunning. Sweaty — but stunning. Her long eyelashes hooded her honey-colored eyes, and specs of freckles dusted just across the bridge of her nose. Her face was flushed and glistening, and I suddenly didn't hate the blazing heat. When I lowered the window, the shock on her face was impossible to miss. She was not expecting me. And I definitely wasn't expecting her.

When Zeke asked me earlier to drive the Maverick back to the owner, I couldn't grab the keys fast enough. At that point, everyone knew my obsession with it. I personally went over the hotrod inside and out at least three times, making sure everything was as it should be. And it is. That car is fucking perfect. Rebuilt 302 CID V-8 engine, original undercarriage, chrome bumpers, high back Grabber black vinyl seats.

It's strong, resilient, special. The fact that someone could so easily throw it away completely blows my mind.

I followed Claire's eyes as they trailed from my face down to my hands suddenly clutching the steering wheel as if it would fly away. Was she judging my tattoos? She wouldn't be the first. Not that I give a shit what anyone else thinks. Only for some reason, I kind of do care what *she* thinks. What the hell is that about?

I got out of the car and she started talking, rambling really, but all I noticed was how her full lips moved and the way she smelled sweet but mild. Like vanilla? Holy shit, something's wrong with me.

Thank God I've mastered the art of masking my emotions so she couldn't see the betrayal I felt by my thoughts. I answered with clipped responses, only expanding when I explained why I was there in place of Zeke. When I offered her the keys, I caught her looking at my tattoos again. Only it wasn't judgment that I saw in her eyes. I think it was more like admiration.

It was only when she asked *my* name that I felt the immediate urge to know hers — to label the anomaly that was somehow clouding my thoughts. I am not one to ever notice women. I mean, I notice them obviously, but I couldn't care less about approaching them. From what I've experienced, relationships lead to nothing but absolute misery. Love is the last thing I'm looking for. The last thing I'm capable of.

"Claire."

I needed a cigarette immediately. I tried to head out, knowing I could probably smoke at least once in the time it would take to get back to Monroe's, but she insisted on driving me. Honestly, as bad as I needed the nicotine relief, it was fucking hot out, and I could tell Claire was embarrassed by the amount of times she'd asked. Maybe she really was just nice, or maybe this was her charity work for the day, but either way, I put us both out of our misery and agreed to the ride.

And now we're here. Parked in front of the garage, still sitting in silence. I don't typically do small talk but I wish she would say something? *Anything?* Finally, she thanks me for bringing the car, and I exhale a breath I didn't realize I was holding. She looks at me expectantly, but I only nod because apparently, my voice box isn't working anymore. I clear my throat and eventually convince my mouth to open.

"I appreciate the ride back."

I unhook my seatbelt and open the door but pause getting out just long enough to look back at her one more time. She's already watching me, bringing her eyes to meet mine. The moment feels heated, and I can't tell if it's the sudden gust of warmth from the open door or something else. Either way, I shake the feeling. Nothing is happening, not with her or anyone else. Besides, I'll never see her again.

I leave the car, shut the door behind me, and walk into work without looking back.

6

Claire

What the hell was that? I'm pretty sure my brain cells just broke the record for some sort of mental marathon. From the second he got in the car, I couldn't stop my mind from running, which isn't exactly new to me, but interesting for sure.

Should I talk? What would I say? I could turn the radio on, but what if something ridiculous like the Black Eyed Peas is playing? Imagine — Mr. Broody-Toughguy sitting in my passenger seat with his tattoos and cigarettes and *My Humps* starts blasting through the speakers! Besides, he didn't seem too eager to talk to me either. Instead, I kept my mouth shut and my hands at ten and two. It was only when it was speak or die from unbearable silence, that I was able to compel myself to thank him for bringing back the car.

Between that and his exit, it was all just strange. He totally caught me staring at him, but I guess he was also kind of staring at me? Honestly, I'm not sure what just happened. The whole thing was weird.
And intense and arousing.
And just really freaking weird.

I head back to my apartment and shower off the sweat and awkward-ness, making the time now 4 pm. Considering my situation, I scheduled a bunch of extra tutoring sessions this month, and one is today in an hour. Perfect. That leaves forty-five minutes before I have to leave, to sit at my computer and write. First, I throw on a loose dress, so sick of my clothes sticking to me. Then, I pull out my laptop.

I got serious about my writing last Christmas break when I suddenly had some unexpected free time. I thought I'd be spending my break with my boyfriend of ten months, Mark, who was a first-year medical student with a crazy schedule. I left my entire break empty, not one thing on my calendar, so we could spend all of his days off together. Well, those plans changed abruptly when Dr. Mark decided to celebrate night one of Hanukkah by sticking his candle in his floor nurse's menorah. Talk about spreading the light. I can say from experience, *that* one did not burn for eight straight days if you know what I mean. Needless to say, when he showed up at my apartment to tell me he cheated on me, I wasn't all that disappointed. I slammed the door in his face and never talked to him again. So, Mark was done, and therefore I now had a week of break and no plans to fill it.
Thus the writing.

I've always wanted to write professionally. As a teenager, I had a secret dream to write children's books someday, but I realized soon after, that possibly the biggest part of a children's book is the illustrations and despite my skill with words, art is another story. So now, I just write poems, journal entries, and letters. I write short stories from my own life too — things that I want to remember. But what I really want to write is a novel, specifically a young adult book. Teaching middle school has shown me the importance of kids and teens investing in reading, and what better way to get them to buy in than by ensuring they have access to great stories that are relevant to their own lives? Now I just have to come up with a life-changing idea.

I'm reading the last two lines of a poem I started yesterday when I realize I'm thinking about *him*.

> *You flow over peaks and run down the mountains.*
> *You glisten in heat while bursting through fountains.*

Apparently, water is now sexual, and *I* am insane. I don't even know this guy. Not to mention, we look like absolute opposites, and the vibe he was putting out didn't exactly scream, *"I'm interested."*

I slam my laptop shut. I think that's enough writing for today. I check the clock — 4:26 pm. Good enough. It takes fifteen minutes for me to get to the library and set up my space in the tutoring center. That leaves just enough time for me to grab a coffee on the way.

7

Jamison

I park my truck and walk around the side of the strip mall where Enzo's sits in the middle. Normally I would go through the back, which leads right to my apartment, but I skipped lunch to look over the Maverick, and I am starving for a couple of slices.

I grab a smoke from my pack as I stride toward my destination. Back, forth, back, I rub it habitually between my lips before it settles in its familiar spot, waiting to be lit. My lighter barely hits the tip when I hear someone mumble something from behind me. Instinctively I snap my head back searching for the source.

"I said, you should quit."

Standing in front of me are the same amber eyes from this morning. The same loose waves, this time down, falling in damp ripples around her face. The same lashes, same freckles, and dammit if it isn't the same full lips, only now they're pursed around a straw. Nerves that haven't been lit in a long time spark to life at just the sight of her mouth in that shape. What the hell is she doing here? And why do I care?

Drawing a long drag for effect, I blow the smoke discreetly from the corner of my mouth, away from where she's standing.

"I'm not much, but I'm definitely not a quitter, Claire."

She smiles with her mouth still sipping her drink. The satisfaction I get from that smile is embarrassing. Between that and the sundress she must have changed into between our first meeting and now, my mind and body seem completely mesmerized by this girl that I don't even know. I'm not sure if it's exhaustion or hunger but it's like I don't have enough energy to pretend I don't care. It goes against everything in me, but I play along.

"Are you stalking me now?" I deadpan. This time she pulls back completely from her straw.

"Excuse me? First, you show up at *my* dad's house and now you walk right past *me*. I was here first so if anything..." It hits her that I'm kidding just a little too late. "Very funny."
There's that smile again.

I puff my cigarette again as my reward and lift my head to release the smoke. Looking back down our eyes meet and suddenly nothing feels funny. Well, actually something feels pretty fucking funny, just not my stupid joke.

"So," she says to break our stare, "What are you doing over here?" She gestures to the strip of stores and restaurants behind us.

Flicking my ash, I buy myself half a second then motion to Enzo's.

"Just grabbing food after work." It's technically not a lie. *Plus I live there.*

"Oh, Enzo's! I've never been there, but I hear it's good."

"Best in town." Again, not a lie. *Plus I live there.*

"I'll have to try it sometime." She pauses expectantly. I realize she's waiting for me to reciprocate the question. Damn, is this what casual conversation is?

"How about you? Since apparently you're *not* following me?"

She tilts her head and squints as if to say, "Ha Ha" then shakes her iced coffee.

"Busy's." She points to the sign on the door right behind us where BUSY BREWZ is written in bold yellow lettering.

"With a 'Z.' Cute." I puff again, poorly attempting to hide my smirk.

She rolls her eyes playfully and my stomach rolls with them. My own body is betraying everything I've ever known.

"The butterscotch latte is my weakness," she laughs but I'm immediately hit with a memory.

I'm five and in my closet, blanketed by dirty laundry. My palm hurts and I don't know why. There was screaming and banging in the next room, so I stopped playing with my Matchbox cars and did what Mommy told me to do — I'm hiding until she comes to get me. I don't know how long I've been here, but all of a sudden, I hear the closet door creep open.

"Jamison, it's okay, honey. Mommy's here." I hear her knees hit the floor.

The sound of her voice alone is enough to calm me down. Suddenly my palm doesn't hurt so bad. I crawl out from under the clothes and into Mommy's arms. Her shirt is ripped and she smells like him, but she hugs me tight and gently kisses the top of my head.

"It's okay. It's okay," she says over and over and over. When I finally let go, she wipes silent tears from my cheeks. "I brought you something." My face lights up. "Close your eyes and put out your hand." I do as she says.

When I open, I see a small butterscotch candy sitting next to my red 1979 Lincoln Continental. I smile, then she smiles, and we both ignore that the spot where it sits on my hand is surrounded by tiny red indents matching the car's frame.

I blink hard and Claire is staring at me, head slightly forward, waiting.

"Sorry, what did you say?"

"I said, have you ever had one?" she repeats, raising her cup.

"Oh, uh, no. Not really my thing." If she notices my dejection she doesn't react.

"They're kind of sweet, but they taste like childhood."

"Yeah, that's the problem," I mutter under my breath, looking at the ground to stomp out my butt before throwing it away.

"What was that?"

"I should probably go." Shoving my hands in my pockets, I meet her gaze. She's caught off guard by my sudden exit, but I think it's best I end this now.

"Oh, sure, yeah, me too," she says, checking her watch.

I tighten my lips and walk backward two steps before turning around completely. As I reach Enzo's I glance over my shoulder, but Claire is gone.

"Jay! Where the hell ya been?" Ronan Caruso stretches a large pizza dough, then throws it high above his head. He stands behind the counter, his short frame half hidden by the display window filled with pies of all different toppings from extra cheese to eggplant florentine. His shirt, dusted in flour says: **May I Suggest the Italian Sausage** with a suggestive arrow pointing towards his apron. The humor is so unlike him that it makes it even funnier.

The best part is that Ro isn't even Italian. The kid is as pale and Irish as they come, but the couple that took him in when he was fifteen was. His adopted dad, Enzo, taught him all about the business.

We met when I was twelve and Ronan was fourteen. There was a brief two weeks that we shared the same foster house where I was coming and he was going. In those two weeks we formed a quiet bond, sharing space with four other younger kids and sneaking glances of disgust at the dinner table — too many times a week, dinner was bowls of mushy noodles covered in a thick brown gravy. Fortunately for Ro, there was only one other foster house between this one and the one he ended up calling home.
We weren't all that lucky.

Ronan ladles a heaping spoonful of red sauce onto the stretched dough and smoothes it in circles until it covers the surface. "Haven't seen you on this side of the building in a few days, man."

"I know, I've been covering extra shifts at the garage and am just so beat after. I come home, eat, work out, pass out, repeat."

"Tough, man. Are we still on for next Friday? You can't bail on me now. I need a break from these four fucking walls." He swings his arms around, a drop of sauce falling to the floor.

Ronan and I don't get out very much. There's just a lot of work and a lot less play. It's how we were brought up, or lack thereof maybe for some of us, but every once in a while, we force ourselves to do something social. Friday's plan is a dive bar across town for live music and a few drinks.

"I'll be there," I nod. "But I'll be coming from work so Sean and I will meet you."

"Sounds good." He reaches for a plate and grabs a slice of pepperoni and a slice of mushroom from the display — my usual order. He pulls open the pizza oven and tosses the slices inside to heat up, handing me a cup to fill at the fountain while I wait. I fill my cup halfway with ice and then hit the button for my drink of choice. I breathe in the scent of the root beer as it leaves the machine. A little bit sweet and a little bit spicy, with just a subtle hint of...vanilla.

8

Claire

It has been four days since I ran into Jay — twice — and already, I can't stop my brain from looping our interactions. We don't live in a super small town. Okay, Maple Grove is basically a few quiet neighborhoods, the main strip where Enzo's is, and another set of streets with a few businesses, shops, or restaurants sprinkled about, but it's not *that* small. So, the fact that I have now seen this guy two times in one day seems a little fated. Have I seen him before today? I definitely would have noticed if I had, wouldn't I? All I know is it's like this orange car came to town and knocked our very average-sized universe right off of its axis.

For the last ninety-six hours, I have tried to occupy my mind — tried to think of something else, anything else, besides him, but it's like even in our short interactions, he's left his mark. Why? I'm not entirely sure, considering both ended pretty horrendously, but my brain doesn't seem to care if he was interested or not.

I put on chapstick, and I picture the way Jay brushed the end of his cigarette across his lips as he walked past me at Busy's. I read, and the main male character suddenly has hazel eyes and tattoos despite how the author's description. It doesn't help that a mix of menthol and motor oil still sits in my car, so I can't even go anywhere without a reminder of him. Since when are cigarettes and engine grease the opposite of gross?

By now I have completely exhausted all attempts at distracting myself on my own. So, I text the only person I can think of that could possibly help. Either she will entertain me to the point of forgetting, or she will meet my level of crazy and join me in fixating on everything that happened.

ME: Movie and takeout?

CHLOE: God, yes! Come over?

ME: On my way.

Why can't all interactions be this simple?

Chloe is already an hour into *Armageddon* when I get to her apartment. She's sitting in the corner of the couch, *her* spot, with a bun on top of her head and fuzzy Christmas socks on her feet. She's wrapped in her favorite cheetah print blanket, a glass of red wine half-full in her hand.

"I was already watching when you texted. We can call for food in a minute," she says without looking away from the screen.

"Starting early?" She looks at me and I point to the glass in her hand.

"It's my first one. You know how I get when Ben sings to Liv before he leaves. Plus, it's really not that early." She's right on both accounts. She sobs when Ben Affleck belts out *Leaving on a Jet Plane* while holding Liv Tyler before he enters the shuttle and it is 3 pm. I have seen Chloe consume alcohol at such early hours of the day that it makes her drink look like a nightcap.

I walk over to *my* spot on the couch, the side with the chaise, and shove my now bare feet under the lip of her blanket. This is good. I feel better. I'm cozy, with my best friend, and watching a group of drillers plan to stop an asteroid from destroying all mankind. What could be better than this? I'm already thinking of so many things that aren't...what's his name again?

Chloe pauses the movie right before the song and turns to me. "Okay, before this gets started. What's up?"

"What do you mean?" I ask.

"I mean, we have been off for like two weeks now and until today you have been Miss. I-Have-Tutoring or Miss. I-Have-Laundry or Miss. I-Have-to-Think-of-the-Next-Little-Women."

"Little Women?" I interrupt. "Really?"

"You know what I mean. This is the first time you have wanted to make a plan to do something fun. So," she sips her wine, "What's up?"

I purse my lips. I met Chloe during open interviews at Jefferson. We graduated college the same year, with the same degree, and bonded quickly over our love of caffeine and matching JCrew pencil skirts. Following the interviews, I was fortunate enough to secure a contract in my own classroom and Chloe got hired as an instructional assistant. Luckily for both of us, she was assigned to three rooms, one of which was mine. It was pretty much grunt work for eight hours a day but now she has a job she loves, teaching reading support at the elementary school two towns over. Turns out the whole position was just a stepping stone for her. Thankfully our friendship was more permanent than that.

We haven't known each other all that long, but our friendship is the type that feels like we've been friends forever. From the very start, we were close. We quickly developed inside jokes and bad habits of oversharing about everything. Me texting her when I had a suspicious rash and her sending me unsolicited dick pics she got from guys she was texting. When people meet us they assume we're childhood friends. We just get each other, which is why she knows now that something is up.

"Nothing," I say almost too casually, but I am determined to not open the floodgates by bringing up He-Who-Shall-Not-Be-Named.

"Liar," she says matter-of-factly, sipping on her wine.

"I am not!"

"You are too. You're making the same face you made before we were friends and I wore those red leather pants and you told me they looked very *Oops!...I Did It Again.*

"Well, they did look very Britney," I say.

"Yeah! Like shave her head and smash a car window, Britney!" The wine in her hand sloshes as she mimics the infamous scene.

"Those pants were terrible," I admit.

"Well, I know that now. But had I known your face three years ago, I would have known it then too."

"Okay!" I blurt out because, honestly, I am too weak to hold it in any longer. "I met a guy."

"You met a guy?"

"I met a guy."

She flicks off the TV and turns her whole body toward me, sitting up so she is in her *I'm really listening* stance.

"He works at Monroe's. He dropped the Maverick off when I was at Dad's."

"Ooh, a mechanic. Good with his hands." She winks and I ignore her.

"I drove him back to the garage in possibly the most uncomfortable silence. But then I saw him again on my way to the library yesterday."

"A mechanic that reads?" She asks, her face tilted.

"No, I was getting a coffee and he was smoking outside."

"Ah, a mechanic that smokes. Now that makes way more sense." She nods her head like all is right again in the world.

"Correct. And I don't know what it is, but I can't seem to shake him."

Chloe lets out an ear-piercing squeal. "Claire! This is so exciting!"

I roll my eyes and lean back in my seat. "It's really not."

"I'm serious!" she continues. "You haven't even talked about a guy since what's his name."

"Mark," I say.

"Right, since what's his name latka-ed the hell out of some other girl's potatoes."

"I'm pretty positive that makes absolutely no sense," I say.

"You know what I mean. This is great! Now I get to hear about your guy stuff for once." Chloe has been going on horrible date after horrible date for quite a while, and although it's fun hearing about her misfortunes, I'm sure she appreciates some reciprocation on the subject.

"Well, don't get too excited. He barely knows I exist."

She grabs her phone from the end table. "Well, that's fine. We'll just—"

"He doesn't have social media," I interrupt. "I checked." It wasn't my finest moment going all crazy-girl detective, but around hour forty-eight, I had to do something.

"Not what I'm doing," she says and now I'm the one who gets into my *I'm really listening* stance because what else could she possibly be looking for?

"Got 'em!" She yells after another few seconds.

"Got what...?"

She stands and slides out of her fuzzy socks and into her flip-flops. "The hours of one, Monroe's Motors." My lips part but I'm not even really sure what to think let alone say.

"Come on silly!" She calls from the kitchen, grabbing her keys off the counter. "I think I'm due for an oil change."

9

Jamison

I hear the car pull into the parking lot before I see it. A pop song about jets blares from the stereo and the tires screech as they turn into the first spot in the lot. A petite blonde girl with her hair in a mess on top of her head throws open the driver's side door and steps out in flip-flops. All of the guys look up, if only because of the hurricane that just blew in, but it doesn't hurt that she's female and definitely attractive. She walks over to the front desk where Zeke, who was once half-asleep, is now fully awake in his chair.

I round the side of the car I'm dealing with in time to listen to the girl ask if we, "Do oil changes and stuff like that," and hear Zeke laugh in response. Where most of us find this type of ignorance kind of annoying if we're honest, he finds it endearing being that his own daughter who practically grew up here, doesn't know a thing about cars. Zeke dives into a list of all of the basic maintenance and repairs we offer — oil changes, filter replacements, battery checks, tire rotations — and the girl nods along like it's the most interesting thing on Earth.

I turn to leave them to their conversation and get back to my work, when I see from the corner of my eye, one long, lean leg pop out from the passenger side of the blonde girl's car. Another foot meets the ground and before my head interprets who it is, my body knows. A sudden head rush and sweaty palms cause me to drop the wrench in my hand and it pulls the figure's eyes to mine. Claire.

Ever since I passed her near Enzo's, I can't seem to shake her. I'm clearly attracted to her, that much is obvious, but there's something else about her that interests me. Maybe it's the fact that she's not throwing herself at me like some girls who go off only looks, or maybe it's that my lack of enthusiasm for conversation doesn't seem to stop her from trying. Either way, ever since walking away from her after the butterscotch incident, I've had this gnawing in my chest that's pretty close to regret, a feeling I am all too familiar with. Now, she's in front of me again. I pick up the wrench, deciding on my next move.

Unlike her friend, her presence is quiet. No one else so much as even looks up, but I can't look away. She stands behind the open door, holding the frame on top with one hand. She offers me a small wave, and I smack the wrench against my palm to make sure I'm not dreaming. This girl who has occupied my mind for the last four days is standing in front of me. The girl I have pictured in my bed, in the shower, in the car, on her knees...here.

I grab a rag from my back pocket and slide the wrench into its place. Wiping grease from my hands, I focus my eyes on the space between my fingers and make my way to her. When I reach the car, our eyes meet, her lips parting and then quickly closing again. She inhales a deep breath and drops her head, nervously tucking her hair behind her ear. My body responds to fucking everything this girl does. She waves, and I feel it in my gut, she parts her lips and I lick mine, she touches her hair, and I picture it wrapped around my goddamn fist.

I want to speak, but I'm not good at this. Not good at talking to anyone, let alone someone I've seen more in my fantasies than in real life, and definitely not the first person who has caused this kind of response in me for as long as I can remember. I search my brain for something to say to break the tension, willing my voice to speak.

"So just to clarify, you *aren't* stalking me?" I say.

She takes a second to think then replies, "What's your definition of stalking?"

I laugh unexpectedly, a reaction so strange to me, and she raises an eyebrow in response, pleased with herself.

"How about, what are you doing here?"

"My friend needs her oil changed." She says it quickly like she's trying to convince herself rather than me. "Do you do those here?" She immediately closes her eyes like she's embarrassed that the question slipped out.

I make a point of looking around the garage that is filled with cars and all things related. "We do."

"Good," she says awkwardly. "Her lucky day." *My lucky day*, I think. She looks down at the rag, and I realize I've been wiping my hands this entire time. I shove the towel back into my pocket and pull out a cigarette.

"This okay?" I ask, holding it out. She nods but looks off in the distance, and I can feel the space she internally puts between us.

"Sorry, I'm not that good at this," I say.

"Smoking?"

"Talking."

She blushes. I bring the cigarette to my mouth and her eyes trail my movement. When I run the filter over my bottom lip, I swear I hear the slightest gasp escape from hers. She swallows hard, her eyes coming back to mine. I'm reminded of the way they're like maple syrup, in color and context, pulling mine to hers and sticking them in place.

"Get to Enzo's yet?" I ask to distract myself from the reel my mind plays of all of the ways I'd like to make her breathe that noise again.

"It's on my to-do list," she says.

I take a long drag, hold it, and exhale, all without breaking eye contact. She shifts her weight from one foot to the other, pulling her hair to one shoulder revealing much more skin than I'm capable of right now.

I catch myself staring at the curve below her neck and force my gaze back upward. "What else is on your *to-do* list, Claire?" She makes that sound again and I feel it between my fucking legs. Is it possible for one girl to completely change the DNA of an entire grown man?

Her friend returns to the car at either the *least* or *most* convenient time.

"Welp," she says. "Never mind! Turns out I'm all set."

We both look at her like we have no idea what that means and again, I'm conflicted. I *want* her to stay, but I *need* her to go.

Her friend winks at her and slides into the driver's side. Claire puts one foot inside the car but hesitates before moving the rest of her body.

"Maybe I'll see you around then," I say, and fuck, do I mean it.

"Now who's the stalker?" She pulls her other leg inside and closes the door and I watch them drive away.

10

Claire

Pushing open the door, I call out to my parents that I'm here. It's always weird announcing myself in the house I lived in for eighteen years, but God forbid I scare my parents by arriving on time for the dinner we eat together every week. If I had a dollar for every *"Heaven's sake, Claire!"* I've gotten, I'd be loaded. So much in fact, that I may be saved from the current problem at hand.

I've spent the last few days reeling from Chloe's little charade. When I asked her on the car ride home what her intentions were, she assured me that it was important that you remind men that you exist.

I then said something along the lines of *"I'm pretty sure if I have to remind a man that I am alive, that's probably not a great sign of compatibility,"* to which she replied, *"Claire, you highly underestimate the stupidity of men."*

Regardless, if any part of her wanted to solidify my unhealthy obsession with a man I barely know, she was extremely successful. It's like he was an itch I couldn't scratch that's now threatening to kill me. Like when you're starving so you eat a snack only to realize now you're even hungrier than before, that one small taste only deepening the need.

"In here!" Mom calls from the kitchen. I hear her chopping lettuce for a salad. Dad's voice comes muffled through his office door, which tells me he's on a late call, as usual.

"Hello, Mother." I quip, offering her a kiss and a box with *Whisk!* written across the top. "Your favorite."

"You're sinful," she says teasingly, holding the blondies from the nearby bakery. Bringing the box to her nose she breathes deeply before setting it off to the side. She sweeps the lettuce into a bowl and begins slicing up a cucumber. I take the first slice and pop it in my mouth as I make my way to the other side of the island for a stool.

"You know, Margie from church told me her grandson is starting at your school in the fall. Sixth grade! Isn't that something?"

"Sure is," I say, swiping another cucumber.

"Do you think you'll have him in one of your classes?"

"No idea. They don't put out the schedules until later so..." I attempt a subject change. "Dad working?"

"You know him. He said he just had to finish some things up for a file and he'd be right out." She glances over. "Speak of the devil himself." Mom throws a wink towards the office door as my dad steps through it.

Dad always seems to be working. When I was younger, he tried his best to make all my silly, school concerts and little, dance recitals despite his busy schedule. He may have snuck in the back a time or two, but he caught at least most of them. He knew what it was like to feel overlooked, so despite the demands of his job, he did his best with the time that he had. That being said, that time was often short.

It helps that Mom, on the other hand, would come early, with bright eyes and a big smile, and sit with whoever she knew at that event, cheering me on, front and center. She never seemed to mind bearing the load of doing almost everything else, as long as he showed up for the big things.

"Your father makes the money Claire!" she used to say. *"I make the magic."* And although she was teasing, she was right. She was the one leaving little notes in my lunches or decorating my door for birthdays, but Dad kept the family afloat in the quiet ways — the ways kids never seem to notice.

"Hey, Claire Bear. Ooh, you brought blondies." Dad per usual heads straight for dessert and tries cracking open the box, as Mom, per usual, smacks his hand simultaneously. "Worth a shot," he says, rounding the island and kissing the top of my head before taking the stool next to mine.

"Claire and I were just talking about Margie's grandson going to Jefferson this year, weren't we Claire."

"Mhmm, sure were," I say spinning my stool away from the counter. "I'll set the table!" Leaving no room for argument, I grab three dishes from the cabinet and head towards the dining room.

"Don't forget the napkins!" my father calls after me, shrugging only to my mom.

I successfully avoid talking about this upcoming school year until dessert when Dad says, "I bet you're anxious to get your normal routine back aren't ya, Bear?"

"Well, it's only been a few weeks, but so far I'm enjoying the summer. I've had a lot of extra time to run and work on my writing. I kind of wish I had more time to do both all year round." I play with the crumbs on my plate waiting for what's coming.

"Those are fun hobbies, sure, but you have to make a living!" He chuckles, wiping first his mouth and then his hands with his napkin.

"Well, although I'm not so sure about the running," I take a sip of water, my throat suddenly dry, "You can make a decent living off of writing, you know? There are journalists and bloggers," I pause to take another sip. "Authors."

I've approached this topic before, casually dropping bait to see if he'd bite. *"Oh, you remember so and so? They write for a food blog now"* or *"Blah blah who went to high school with me, she was published in a magazine."* Every time it's the same response as the one he gives now.

"Sure, those jobs exist but they're for people who didn't get a real degree like you!" Of course, this is wildly untrue, which is the one thing Dad chooses *not* to be factual about. In this case, I think his opinion on the topic clouds his otherwise factual mentality. His opinion being that

I was born to be a teacher and so a teacher is what I'll be. So, despite that millions of successful authors do exist and make a living through this "hobby," there's no convincing him that *I* could possibly want to be one of them.

He reaches for the box of dessert, but Mom pulls it away. "I'm just saying Claire, you're in a respectable profession."

"Amen!" Mom chimes cheerfully. Always the cheerleader.

"Those kids are lucky to have you!" he says.

"And so are we!" Mom ends the conversation, collecting our plates, taking with her two very important things — the blondies and my dream.

11

Jamison

"In your dreams, man."

I snap the newspaper shut, but Sean is still leaning over my shoulder. The ad for the Maverick was posted this morning, and despite it being way out of my price range, I was curious what the listing said.

"Okay, first of all, get your hot ass breath off of my neck." I shrug making contact with Sean's chin. He staggers back dramatically like he caught an uppercut with a closed fist rather than a tap of my shoulder.

"And second, I was just looking." I fold the newspaper and tuck it under my arm, pulling a new pack of cigarettes from my back pocket. I brush one side to side and settle it on my lips.

"You know you should really quit that," Sean says, rubbing his jaw.

"So I've been told."

"For real though, why torture yourself like that looking in the paper? An ignorant rich guy's gonna pay an arm and a leg to store that thing in his six-car garage so he can show it to people at dinner parties and shit." He stands straight adjusting an imaginary tie, then raises his eyebrows and purses his lips, holding his hand in a C shape.

I pull my hand away from my mouth. "Are you having a stroke?"

"No, I'm the rich guy! See! I'm drinking my cocktail." He repeats the painful expression, only somehow more dramatically this time, before dropping the act altogether.

"Never mind. All I am saying is you're just setting yourself up to be let down."

I exhale. "Whatever, man." Brushing him off, I head into the office to check today's schedule. He's right though. I'm investing way too much time in something that's never going to happen. Setting myself up just to be let down, which is something I told myself I was going to stop doing over a decade ago.

I spent three years in foster care before I decided I was done hoping to be adopted.

It's my twelfth birthday, and I'm packing my bag to head to my fourth home this year. The one I'm leaving has so many kids that they didn't even realize I wasn't going to school. When the principal couldn't get a hold of my foster mom, she called my case manager Mel, and when Mel found out I was skipping more classes than I was attending, that was the end of that.

Everything I own fits into one worn backpack. I toss it into Mel's car and she hands me a cupcake and a lighter.

"Happy birthday, kid."

I have to light my own candle, but it's more than I expected. Mel is good people, but even she has more kids on her caseload than she can handle.

Blowing out the candle, my wish is that this next house will stick and I'll finally have a home.

"This next one will be better," she say as if reading my mind.

It wasn't.

And neither were the next three.

I went to seven schools in seventh grade and never bothered making a birthday wish again.

Work was back-to-back today. Four inspections, two oil changes, a tire rotation, and a new set of brakes. I'm wiped by the time I get back to the apartment, but for my sanity, I have to get a quick workout in. I strip off my work clothes and throw on a pair of gym shorts.

The one pocket of available space I have in this cell of a room is designated for my "equipment." Really, it's just a bench, a set of dumbbells, and a pull-up bar hooked to the back of the bathroom door, but it does the job and it beats paying for a gym membership.

I bang out a quick workout and a few dozen pushups. By the time I'm done, my whole body's exhausted and covered in sweat, so I toss my shorts and boxers into the pile of laundry in the corner and start the shower. As the water falls down my aching back, my mind drifts back to Claire. I'm embarrassed, and confused, by how often this has happened lately, and even more so since she came by this week.

For as long as I can remember I haven't fixated on a woman like this. I am singular almost to a fault. Nobody but me knows this, but I haven't been with a woman in a very long time. Not a relationship, not a date, not even a fucking one-night stand. I've always considered any interaction too much of a risk. Putting yourself — heart, body, or mind — in someone else's hands means willingly exposing yourself to pain.

But despite all of that, there's something about our brief interactions that threatens to consume me. I don't even know this girl and yet I find my breathing ragged just thinking about her. Her walnut-colored hair and the way she looks through me with her golden eyes. Hell, even the way she rambles pulls me in. I want to interrupt her train of thought, pull her close, and brush my palm down her flushed pink cheeks. Use my thumb to trace the freckles that tiptoe over her tanned skin and sweep it across her full fucking lips. My God those lips.

Suddenly any cravings that I buried a long time ago threaten to surface as I remember what her mouth looked like sucking that straw or releasing that single breath that drove me wild. My body pulses at just the thought and I'm overwhelmed with the need to taste her. I try to shake her off. To push her out of my mind and forget about her. But as I'm standing here, the water turns cool, and still I can't get her out of my head.

12

Claire

I wake up emotionally hungover from dinner with my parents. I don't know why I'm surprised. It's the same story every time work comes up. Mom acts as if I am God's gift to the world of education and Dad — well, his daughter went to a real school and got a real degree. She's a teacher, didn't you hear?

It's exhausting.

I said one time in eighth grade that I might want to go into education and my fate was sealed. Mom signed me up to volunteer in the church nursery and to be a junior counselor at Vacation Bible School. Dad took me to every college fair, grabbing brochures and course catalogs from all of the schools known for their education program. Then, every May when it came time to choose classes for the next year, they'd both sit over my shoulder and prompt me to remember the path to teaching!

Ninth grade - Child Development I

Tenth grade - Child Development II

Eleventh grade - Public Speaking

Twelfth grade, forget about it. I was in every advanced placement class they offered so that I could test out of my general education classes and focus on teaching courses.

It was completely draining.

Sometimes I wonder if their excitement was why, after a while, it all started to feel more like a chore than a passion. Like maybe they breathed so much life into my career that they started sucking all of the oxygen from me. They were supportive but suffocating, encouraging but unreasonable. Whatever the case, somewhere around year three at Jefferson, no matter how much I loved helping students, the thrill of it all started to fade.

This is why, when Principal Andrews told me at my yearly review that she was doing away with my classes next fall, instead of being upset, I somehow felt...relieved. I remember my shoulders physically relaxing after she said, *"I'm really sorry, Claire. There's just no need for your position."*

Now, the problem lies in what happens next and how do I break my parents' hearts?

"I can't believe you're spending yet another Friday night in the dusty library." Chloe scrunches up her face midchew like she smells rotten trash rather than the fresh meatball sub she's scarfing down at my desk.

"Says the girl who is spending her Friday afternoon wiping sauce from her face with the back of her hand...unsuccessfully I might add." I shove my laptop in my bag along with my planner, workbook, and notecards.

"It's from Enzo's! And it's so good." She closes her eyes savoring her latest bite.

I pause where I'm at. *"What else is on your to-do list, Claire?"*

"Enzo's." I say it aloud unintentionally.

"Yep! Great food. And the short king behind the counter looked equally delicious if I do say so myself." She winks at me, wrapping up her now empty sub paper.

"You'd think a mannequin looked delicious if it had a penis and handed you a sandwich."

Shrugging, she agrees. "You're probably right." We both laugh. Chloe seems to be on a mission lately to find a boyfriend. *"Not a husband, but a boyfriend."* Her words, not mine. That recently has meant flooding her phone with these new dating apps and enjoying free meals with who-ever she matches.

I check the clock – 7:05 pm.

"I'm just saying," she turns to me, this time more seriously. "It's okay for you to go out every once in a while. I mean, when was the last time you spent a Friday night doing something fun."

"Tutoring Zach isn't *not* fun," I say.

"Claire. Zach is a snotty eleven-year-old who probably spends more time staring at your boobs than your workbooks. I think you'd both survive a Friday night without him snickering every time you tell him you're going to dick-tate his spelling words."

"Okay, first, ew." I shiver for effect. "Two, I need the money now more than ever. I have no idea what I am doing once summer ends, and I can't afford to cancel these sessions. Zach's parents pay me a fortune."

"That's because their kid is FOUL," Chloe emphasizes.

"And THREE," I say, mimicking her volume. "I always stay after and get some writing done. It's nice to change up the scenery."

"Listen, Claire, I get it. But can you promise me you'll at least think about leaving the house one of these weekends?" She looks my outfit up and down. "In something you can't also wear to mow the lawn?"

I follow her trail, looking down at my ripped, loose-fitting jeans, and faded Jefferson tank top I ordered from the Spirit Wear sale my first year. Okay, she has a point there. But I like my Friday nights. I like that after suffering through thirty minutes with Zach, who really is pretty foul, I get an envelope of cash and the rest of the night with just me, my thoughts, and a vending machine full of snacks.

I look at the clock again - 7:11 pm.

"Okay, I have to go. My session starts at seven-thirty."

"Fine. I'll get out of here. But think about what I said. And maybe grab a sweatshirt. That tank top is doing nothing to ward off preteen eyes." She wiggles her eyebrows as she throws her balled-up trash toward the garbage can. She misses of course and saunters out the door.

I grab my bag and sling it over my shoulder. I add my laptop charger to it, and because now Chloe has me feeling self-conscious, I throw a hoodie in too. Just in case.

13

Jamison

Riveʼs Rum is packed. Sunday through Thursday itʼs usually just a handful of locals blowing off steam after work, but every Friday and Saturday they host live music and half-price car bombs. Unfortunately for me, Ronanʼs favorite metal cover band, which he met through the pizza business, is playing tonight and despite his denial, he is Irish through and through. So, here we are.

I'm nursing my second whiskey and water when the band hits the stage signaling itʼs 9 pm. Most of the crowd flooding the front bar makes its way to the cheap stage in the back of the small dining area. When there's a band, Riverʼs clears the few tables they have for eating so thereʼs room for people to gather in front of the stage. Tonight itʼs pretty full of loyal fans.

The lead singer announces the band - **Rage Against the SUPREME**. It never gets old, especially because I get to remind Ronan every time we hear it, that I had to explain the significance to him the first time they met.

"I donʼt get it," Ronan said above the noise at the first concert they invited him to.

"Like the pizza Ro...Supreme." He nodded slightly but I knew he was still clueless. They were halfway into the second song when he turned to me, screaming over the sound.

"Jay! Like the toppings!"

Like I said, not Italian in the slightest.

The crowd cheers as the band members mess around, tuning their instruments. Ronan taps my shoulder.

"I'm taking a leak and then heading to the stage. I assume you're staying back here?" He knows me too well.

I raise my drink in answer. He rolls his eyes as he turns away. Ro is like a brother but in most ways, we are nothing alike. He has been through some shit, but he's resilient as hell. An outsider would probably assume that's because he got adopted at fifteen, after being in foster care for just a few months, where I bounced around from shithole to shithole until I aged out of the system. An outsider just may be right.

I watch him walk towards the bathroom where I see Sean now sits at a high-top, embarrassingly close to a punk-rock redhead who is, unbeknownst to him, very clearly uninterested. From the stage, the guitarist starts with the intro to Led Zeppelin's *Stairway to Heaven*.

I scan the bar. Luckily most of its inhabitants fled towards the band, so I grab an empty stool and set down my drink. The few people that are left hold light conversations with the friends they're sitting with. The bartender, a pale woman with jet-black hair and an eyebrow piercing, wipes the counter from the previous rush.

Across from me sits an older couple, probably in their fifties, holding hands in a comfortable silence just listening to the music. She looks around, people watching, swaying to the beat. He sits, one hand on hers, the other on the back of her chair, singing along. It makes me wonder. How do some people end up like that and others end up covered in blood and their own vomit, half in the bag and half in the ground? I throw back what's left of my drink in one large gulp.

Next to me stands a tall skinny dude in a basketball jersey leaning over the stool on his other side. From his body language, I assume he is whispering into the ear of its occupant. His body shifts, and I notice the hand holding his drink tighten around the bottle. The voice of his neighbor grows louder, and I now know it's a woman. Larry Bird over here slams his beer on the counter and pulls her stool so it's all but on top of his, zero to one hundred. The woman's nervous yelp is all I need to hear to confirm my suspicions. I grab this loser's shoulder and snap him around so he's now facing me. His beer flies from his hand and lands in a crash on the floor.

"Bro! What the hell?" he yells.

I snatch the collar of his douchey jersey and pull him so we meet, chest to chest. Speaking in a fierce, low tone, I look him dead in the eye, my face so close to his that the tips of our noses all but touch.

"If I see you so much as look at her wrong, or any other woman for that matter, I will palm your head like a basketball and dribble it down this bar. Got it...bro?"

Before he can respond, we're interrupted by Ronan who caught the whole thing on his way out of the bathroom. Bear-hugging me from behind, he pulls me backward. Reluctantly, I release the now-stretched collar of Basketball-Guy, who huffs, adjusting his jersey. I back up just enough to ease the tension between us.

"You're lucky!" He spits, magically now having something to say. The woman behind him, who until now was frozen, staring wide-eyed, flinches and backs away from him completely.

Assholes like him are all the same. I've seen it my whole life. They're really tough as long as the person they're beating on is weaker than them. They're controlling, abusive, violent — a total fucking waste of space.

I make a quick step toward him as if I'm coming for him again. He springs back like the pussy I know he is, and I laugh in his face. "Luck has nothing to do with it," I reply soberly. Then I turn and walk away. He's not even close to worth it.

"I'm leaving," I say to no one in particular.

Sean, who has now joined Ronan after noticing the commotion, claps me on the back. "You okay, man?"

I bob my head swiftly, throwing cash on the bar to settle my tab. I just want to get out of here, grab a slice, and go to fucking bed. Another hand squeezes my shoulder.

"We good?" This time it's Ro checking in.

"Yeah, but I'm out of here. I'll catch you guys later."

Ronan gives me a knowing nod. Looking at Sean, he points to where the band is starting their next song. Knowing I just need my space, the two head towards the crowd. The familiar drumbeat of Ozzy Osbourne's *Crazy Train* booms from the stage. I pause, taking in the instrumentals and a few deep breaths. When I finally feel like I can pass *Bro* on his stool without going round two, I make my way towards the exit. The woman, who was once by his side, is now at the opposite end of the bar. She gives me an easy smile that speaks volumes. *"Thank you."*

Stepping into the evening heat, the sound of the band resonates outside, while the lyrics play in my head. Walking to my truck, I think about all of the times someone saw my mom in those same situations. Did anyone ever do anything about it? And if they did, did it make her think about changing?

I'm old enough now to know that it's not as simple as just leaving. That people don't just quit drinking or leave abusive relationships on a whim. That the process is grueling and involves danger, risk, and consequences. It's not something you do casually, but a decision you make every single day. That I understand.

What I can't wrap my head around is why I was never enough of a reason for her. Not at six or eight or twelve or fifteen. I drive myself nuts wondering. *Why couldn't she ever just pick me?*

14

Claire

It turns out that Chloe creepily insisting on me wearing layers was actually helpful. The library air was on full blast tonight, but thanks to my hoodie, I managed to survive. I ended up staying for almost an hour after my session with Zach and even managed to brainstorm a few ideas for a novel. It was so surreal even putting them on paper — like songs of my dreams being played out loud.

The only reason I left was because they were closing at nine. That, and my stomach was growling so much they probably would have kicked me out anyway. The vending machine, which is usually stocked with everything from Chex Mix to PopTarts, was severely lacking tonight. Apparently, all of the moms bringing their kids to story times throughout the day have no respect for us grown-ups who need ample amounts of processed sugars to exist.

So, when I was driving past the strip mall, I didn't necessarily make a conscious decision to stop at Enzo's so much as I was pulled there by the forces of fresh sauce and gooey mozzarella cheese. Between Jay and Chloe, it must have been practically brainwashed into my mind because suddenly I was parallel parking a little ways from the building. Before I even thought it through, I shoved my phone in my front pocket and my wallet in the back and headed towards the restaurant.

As weird as it sounds, I smell him before I see him. In reality, the mix of tobacco and mint could have been anyone, but somehow, I knew it was Jay. Leaning with his foot propped and his back against the wall, he still stands over six feet tall. He's wearing dark denim jeans and a black t-shirt that tugs across his chest, sleeves clinging to his biceps like the two things are welded together. He's staring off again, like I've already seen before. Either into space or at the ground, it's like his head is somewhere else. What is it that his mind is always running to? Or maybe running from.

I clear my throat in my subtle attempt to get his attention. He glances at me without breaking his serious exterior and drops his sight back down to the sidewalk he was staring at. From there, his eyes begin to move slowly up my legs. They stop at my waist, then continue up my torso, and suddenly I wish I would have at least left my hoodie in my car. Finally, his exploration continues to my face, pausing I notice, just a beat longer on my lips. It's only when our eyes meet that the intensity of his face softens just a little, the corners of his mouth turning upward so slightly you might miss it if you weren't paying attention. Luckily for me, I was definitely paying attention — to everything about him.

"Claire." Despite my warm clothing, I feel goosebumps form as my body remembers the effect he has on me by just speaking my name. "What did we say about stalking?"

"Jay." I surprise myself with my quick reaction. "What did we say about quitting?" I gesture towards his half-smoked cigarette. "Plus, I'm not stalking, just starving, and someone said this is the best pizza in town." Pointing to the neon sign in the window I add, "Please tell me they're still open."

"For..." He pulls his phone from his pocket, and I can see from the screen the time reads 9:18 pm. "Twelve minutes." He puts his cigarette out on the wall and trashes the butt, then nods his head towards the door.

There's a slight panic that crawls up my body as I realize he's asking if I want to go in — with him. Considering I just miraculously showed up here, I didn't think I might see him. Had I, I definitely would have done my makeup and ditched the oversized college hoodie for a school I didn't even attend. I catch my reflection in the window and wince. Yep, that's a cheese curl stain from my subpar vending machine purchase earlier this evening. Curse the little rats who stole all of the PopTarts. A Frosted Brown Sugar Cinnamon would never have let me down like this.

Without waiting for my response, Jay pulls back the door to Enzo's and holds it open for me to pass through, his tattoos on full display. Because suddenly I'm sweating, I quickly strip off my hoodie and tie it around my waist before moving through the door.

The perfect combination of fresh basil and fried food floods my senses the second I step into the restaurant. The decor is familiar but unique. There's black and white checkered flooring and red leather seat cush-ions, reminiscent of traditional pizza parlors, but the wall art screams one-of-a-kind. Where old-school places might hang pictures of classic doughboys with chef hats and handlebar mustaches, this one has ones of mob bosses and vintage Italian gangsters.

There's a wide serving window right in front displaying a dozen dif-ferent types of pizza. Most of the pies are down to just a slice or two, considering the time, but my mouth still waters at what's left. Behind the window is an open kitchen and to the left are a handful of two-top tables, the majority of which already have their chairs flipped on top of them.

A tan, bearded guy, probably several years older than me, approaches the counter wiping his hands on a shabby dishrag. He's wearing a worn white Enzo's shirt, a dusted black apron, and a scar above his right eye.

"Yo, Jay! I thought you guys were goin' to River's?" the worker says and apparently these two know each other.

"Yeah, we did but I bailed early. Sean and Ro will be there awhile."

"Cool, cool. Can I get you guys somethin'?" He looks from Jay to me, then back to Jay with a look on his face I just can't place. Surprise maybe?

"This is Claire. Claire, Mikey."

He answers Jay with an approving look then speaks in my direction. "Pleasure."

"It's nice to meet you, Mikey."

Ordering for the both of us, Jay says, "We'll take two slices each of whatever you got left." Turning to me he adds in a softer voice, "Don't worry, they're all good."

"You got it, boss. Have a seat and I'll bring 'em right over." Mikey hands him two empty cups and moves to throw the slices in the oven.

I go for my wallet but before I reach it, Jay grabs my forearm gently, pulling it back. My whole body tenses as his hand brands my flesh beneath its touch, but that quickly it's gone as he holds one of the cups out for me to take, the skin where his hand once was, left raw and vacant. Did he feel that too? I shake the curiosity from my mind and follow him to the soda fountain.

I thank him for the pizza looking at my soda choices. I land on 7Up and fill my cup with extra ice.

"Don't worry about it," he replies. "I know the owner." He fills his cup next. I wouldn't have taken him for a root beer guy.

We walk to the closest table that still has both chairs on the floor. I place my wallet on the table so I don't have to sit on it. Jay pulls a now familiar teal box and lighter from his pocket and mimics the movement before taking the seat across from me.

"You know, when people share a meal they usually talk to each other too," I say remembering his *"I'm not good at this"* comment. "Are you sure you're up for that?" I say it sarcastically but the reality is I'm not sure *I'm* up for it.

He leans back in his chair and crosses his arms over his chest. He's not even flexing and his colorful biceps bulge against his fists.

"And what is it that these people tend to talk about?"

"Well, typically they talk about their day or their jobs or things they like. Sometimes it's even more than a dozen words if you can believe it." I raise my eyebrows challenging him. He remains silent for what feels like hours before he finally speaks.

"Okay, smartass." He smiles the most honest smile before regaining his composure and landing in a smirk. "My day was long, my job is fine, and I like classic cars." He pauses. "And you."

My breath hitches at his last two words. *"And you."* We lock eyes. His face is completely serious but the sea of gold and green I'm swimming in tells me he's just as shocked by his confession as I am. Afraid to speak,

I hold our gaze a second longer. It's only when Mikey reaches between us to drop our food, do I dare look down.

"Here you go, amici." He spins one plate in front of Jay and the other to me. "Oh, and Ro texted. He said just lock up when you're done." I look up surprised as Mikey holds a fist out in Jay's direction. I watch him return the gesture, his eyes still locked on me. He breaks the intensity, casting a playful wink in my direction as Mikey heads towards the exit.

"Like I said," he says, "I know the owner."

15

Jamison

Mikey just left but not before I somehow managed to tell Claire I like her and throw her a goddamn wink. Moron. It's like the rock-hard exterior I've worked so hard to build turns to mush in front of this girl. I have never had word vomit like I did just then. The thoughts that came pouring from my mouth were completely outside of my control. My only saving grace is that she didn't seem completely disgusted by either of my impulsive moves.

This whole thing is just really throwing me off. I'm not surprised she gets my attention, I mean look at the girl. But there's something about her that's *keeping* my attention, which is the confusing part. Not to mention, the fact that she showed up here all but one minute after I did after the night I've had, makes me feel like this cold world actually worked in my favor for once. Then, you add that she first initiated conversation and agreed to eat with me, and I'm pretty sure I owe my life to some higher power.

I was replaying the bar incident over in my head earlier when she spoke my name. The tone of her voice alone sent signals to places from inside my gut to under my jeans. This is the first time I've seen her completely hidden by clothes and my body still reacted to the sight of her. When she took off her sweatshirt revealing bare arms and just a shred of cleavage, I all but came undone. For the second time, this girl fucking turned me on just by being herself. Thank God I walked in behind her.

Looking at my two slices, I see Mikey gave me one mushroom and one sausage, which is my second favorite if they're out of pepperoni.

Claire's plate holds one ham and ricotta — an Enzo's specialty — and one Hawaiian.

"That's a bold move for Mikey. Pineapple on pizza is kind of hit or miss." I fold the sausage slice in half and bring it to my lips.

Claire's already a mouthful into the ham and ricotta, but after a few chews, she manages to respond. "Anything on this slice of heaven has to be a hit." She takes another massive bite and the sound she makes should not be sexy. She swallows and takes a sip of her 7Up. "You said you know the owner?"

"Yeah, Mikey's brother, Ronan, has been my best friend since we were young. He opened this place a few years ago. Now he and Mikey run it together."

"Woah, two brothers in business, that could be dangerous." She rips off a piece of crust.

"Nah, they get along great. Wasn't the case at first but once Ro settled in, they were fine."

Brushing the dust from her fingers she questions me. "Settled in?"

"Mikey and Ronan aren't blood brothers. Mikey's parents adopted Ronan when he was fifteen, right before Mikey's seventeenth birthday."

Claire seems to process what I just said and then takes a long sip of soda. After clearing her throat she says, "Wow, being adopted at fifteen had to have been tough. I mean, teenage years are hard enough."

My instinctual response comes to my mind. *Try not being adopted at all.* I don't say it out loud because I can tell she meant no harm by it, but that's always people's reaction to Ronan's story. Don't get me wrong, no one knows how hard it was for him better than I do, but at least he found a new family. I take a large bite of my mushroom slice so she'll think that's why I'm not responding and answer only with a nod.

"Was probably hard for Mikey too." She looks off to the side like she's really thinking about it. She's surprised when a short laugh escapes my lips, so I quickly clarify.

"Mikey was so excited. I had never seen a seventeen-year-old kid so happy about something that wasn't related to boobs or booze." I wipe my mouth before continuing. "But Mrs. Caruso said his birthday wish every year until he was eleven was for a little brother, so I guess it didn't matter that they were five years late, he was still just as pumped."

Claire flashes that smile again, and it's so real I can't help but smile back. She's invested in their story and she doesn't even know them. Because she's clearly enjoying this, and I apparently enjoy making her happy, I continue.

"Ronan, on the other hand, was a bitter kid, pissed at the world, and rightfully so. He had a hard time trusting really anyone. So, when Mikey jokingly tackled him during a game of touch football, like brothers do, Ronan walked over to him and decked him right in the eye."

Claire's mouth drops open and her eyebrows raise. "The scar! I saw that!"

"Yep. Knocked him right to the ground and busted his eyebrow open. The kid needed four stitches. And you know what Mikey did?" She seems part concerned and part amused, but is hanging on to my every word. I take a sip, savoring her attention just a second longer. "He hugged him."

She clutches her heart with both hands. "No."

"Sure did. And they've been fine ever since." I chuckle thinking of two teenage boys embracing while blood drips down between them. "Man, Mikey is so soft."

"Stop it! No he's not! That's sweet!" She leans over the table and smacks the hand still resting on my cup. Just that touch sends shivers down my arm, but that one second of contact wasn't enough.

Changing the subject, she asks, "So, do you have any siblings?"

I pause unsure of how to answer. Do I tell her the truth? That I'm not sure. That I used to almost two decades ago, but I have no idea if he's even still alive. That technically I could have more somewhere too that I don't even know about. I could lie and just say no. Or omit the truth, telling her I have a brother and leave it at that.

My gut tells me to keep it simple. An easy "Nope" and continue the conversation. But looking at her, I can't seem to get it out. The four letters are lodged in my throat threatening to choke me if I don't swallow them down. So much for word vomit.

I realize then, that for some reason, some batshit crazy reason, I want to tell the truth. I want to uncover what's tucked away. Afraid to give too much too fast though and scare her off completely, I settle on a half-truth.

"One half-brother." My voice is quiet and shakier than I mean for it to be. "But I haven't seen him in a really long time."

Sensing the change in mood, Claire leans over the table again, but this time she doesn't smack my hand, she holds it. "I'm so sorry."

That's it. No questions. No prodding for more details. No attempt to fix it. Those three words wash over me, and I realize I didn't know I needed them until right now. I think this is what has been drawing me to Claire. She seems so goddamn genuine. I mean, the girl couldn't even let me walk back to work without begging to give me a ride for Christ's sake. And now, she's fully invested in Ronan's story and apologizing about my brother, which she knows nothing about. The heart of this girl has to be made of pure gold. And that's something I can't say I've seen very much of.

I look back down at our hands and can't help but notice how well they fit together. I give hers a gentle squeeze because it's all the response I can seem to manage.

Thirty minutes later, we are still sitting at the table. My plate is empty as she takes the last bite of her Hawaiian, minus the crust.

In the last half hour, we have covered everything from past times to favorite foods. She runs and writes, I lift and read, and both of us now prefer Enzo's pizza. We discussed a few of my tattoos (yes that's a naked lady and no I don't know her) and the fact that she hates Ugg boots and people who say audiobooks don't count as reading. We even talked about our favorite singers, hers, unfortunately, Pink! and mine a tie between Elton John and Tom Petty, because there's just something about the way they sing that tells a story.

Basically, we have covered a lot of meaningless topics, and I'm not sure I've had a better conversation in my entire life.

At the end of it, I find that I just want all of it again. Another story, another question, another time to have her skin on mine. I could have killed myself for releasing her hand to swat a fly away that must have snuck in, but by the time I realized what I'd done, she had already pulled her arm back across the table to tuck her hair behind her ear.

Dropping her napkin on her plate, Claire brings that same hand to her perfect mouth to stifle a yawn. The last thing I want, which is wild to me, is for our conversation to end, but it is getting late, and I have to be at work at the ass crack of dawn. I collect our trash before I reluctantly say, "I guess we should get out of here."

Standing and stretching, she yawns again. "I think I'm in a pizza coma."

"I told you, best in town."

"Okay, try not to let it go to your head, but you were right. I mean, they were both great, but the pineapple was definitely not a miss." I wipe down our table with a napkin and pile our two chairs on top.

Without thinking of the aftermath I say, "Hawaiian was my mom's favorite." She smiles as she slowly walks towards the exit. I never talk about my mother, let alone to someone that I barely know, but it's out now, and I love how she seems to notice and appreciate when my walls drop even an inch.

This whole idea of sharing is so unfamiliar to me and usually, it's uncomfortable to say the least. But with Claire, I'm like a fucking dog with a bone looking to dig up everything that's buried and lay it at her feet.

"Sometimes, when I was really little, she used to come in after a long night and put a frozen pizza in the oven. Then, right before it was finished cooking, she would pull out the oven rack and open up a can of diced pineapples. She'd hand me some and keep some for herself, and we would take turns throwing them into the oven to try to get them to land on the pizza."

I smile thinking back to good times with Mom for once, but then I remember what I left out — that she would come in after a long night of drinking where she left me alone at home by myself. That she'd pull open the oven rack, exposing her newest set of bruises.

This time I choose omission and leave those parts out. "Anyway, it made a total mess, but it was fun at the time."

We reach the door and she turns to face me. "Your mom sounds like she really loves you." Her tone is so warm that I feel my walls not just fall but collapse.

"She did." I hesitate, then add, "But she loved alcohol and shitty men more."

And there it is. The entirety of my relationship with my mother summed up in a handful of words. Once it's out, it's like an anvil lifted off my shoulders. I'm not sure I have ever said anything like that out loud. Anything so true. So fucking excruciating. Only the people who were by my side as I went through it — Mel, Ronan, Mikey — know this piece of the puzzle. And now it's out there, poured from the darkest part of me, incapable of being put back in.

Claire shortens the space between us, catching me completely off guard. I search her face for any hint of what she's feeling. Her eyes meet mine and they're a cross between hungry and heartbroken. This shouldn't be happening. But then she brings her hand to my cheek, and I involuntarily lean into her touch. My heart rate quickens, and I'm not sure if it's because I want her or because I don't — because a girl like Claire could be tainted by a guy like me.

Standing on her tiptoes, she brings her lips just inches from mine, and the smell of vanilla lights up my senses. She stills, waiting for me to close the gap.

"You don't want someone like me, Claire." It comes out a whisper of instant regret. Her eyes dart to my lips, then back up to meet my sorrowful gaze.

"I think maybe I do." The hand on my cheek slides to the back of my head, and I close my eyes, soaking it in.

Before I can protest again, either to her or myself, our lips crash together. It's urgent and needy. I pull back hesitantly, anticipating Claire's face to show doubt or regret, but all I see is her need for more. She licks her lips, then parts them, inviting me back in, and as quickly as it ends, it's starting again.

Claire reaches for my hair, tugging it gently, as I brush my tongue against her lips. I feel her smile beneath the contact and even when I can't see it, that smile drives me crazy. My tongue sweeps again, only this time, hers meets mine. A growl escapes from the back of my throat, and she pushes her body closer to mine in response. My hands on her hips, I guide her body toward the wall. Her back connects with the drywall behind her, and as she moans quietly into my mouth, my hand begins to vibrate.

We both pause without breaking apart, then instantly begin again. I move my lips to the corner of her mouth, then brush her hair behind her. She gasps when I press my lips to the soft flesh of her neck before her pocket vibrates again. Laying my forehead against hers, I sigh loudly. Breathing heavily, she brings both hands to my chest. I raise my head, dreading what's next.

"I should probably get going anyway?" She says it like a question she wants me to answer.

Everything I feel right now says to drop to my knees and show her exactly how much I want her — all of her. But everything I've felt for years, says to save her from the fucking mess I am.

I move back half a step and sigh again. "Probably."

She nods her head and pushes off of the wall. Holding open the door so she can pass, I feel the familiarity of the same gesture from just an hour before.

The difference is, that just an hour ago, I held the door open to a world of "What-ifs" —
What if she judges me?
What if she doesn't?
What if she hates me?
What if she doesn't?

An hour later and this time I hold the door open to a whole different world. A world of "What nows" —
What now that we talked?
What now that I liked it?
What now that we kissed?
What now that I like her?

Stepping onto the quiet street, Claire turns to face me again. "Thanks for the pizza, Jay." She presses a gentle kiss to my cheek.

In my head, I grab her hand as she goes to leave and pull her into a tight embrace. When I finally let go, I kiss her hard, in the same way I did before. "Thanks for all of it, Claire," I say.

Only I do none of that. I say none of that. Instead, I shove both hands into my pockets and in silence, I watch her walk away.

16

—

Claire

I drop my head to the steering wheel without even starting my car. What. Just. Happened?

This is NOT how I thought fulfilling my hankering for Enzo's would go, but apparently, I satisfied two kinds of cravings tonight. The only problem is, where my stomach is full, my hunger for Jay has only increased. Thanks a lot, Chloe! She sent me one text asking how my "library banger" was going, and then, followed up with a blurry selfie of her at a bar. In the picture, she's holding up an empty glass with the caption: "My date was a weeny so I'm getting drunk off martinis!"

And interrupting the best kiss of my life!

Looking in the mirror I can see him still standing outside of the restaurant. I fiddle with my phone pretending to be extremely interested in whoever may be texting me, but secretly stealing peeks at him in the rearview. Luckily, I'm parked far enough away that he wouldn't be able to see the direction of my eyes in the darkness. He reaches for his pocket and pulls a cigarette from the box he had before. Drawing it to his lips, he does that thing that fascinated me the first time I saw it as he passed me outside of Busy's Brewz. Back, forth, back, he guides it across his lips. If it captivated me before, I'm now completely enamored, knowing what those lips taste like. As he settles it in place, he looks off into the distance. Is he thinking about our kiss too?

It is completely out of character for me to initiate something like that, but it was at that point in our conversation that I realized he was letting me into a place where very few people are granted access. A place that may be dark and traumatic, but that makes him who he is. The knowledge that I was given exclusivity to see him, really see him, turned me on in a way nothing physical ever has. What scares me most is that now that I've cracked a window, I want to bust down the doors. I want to *know* everything, *feel* everything, *touch* everything. And I have a feeling it's a lot more than I realize, both physically and mentally.

I don't know how long I've been sitting here, but it's been long enough that Jay smothers his cigarette under his boot. I'm confused when I see him turn to go back into Enzo's. I immediately think he needs to lock the door, but no, he closes the door while he's still inside. Maybe he forgot something? I decide he must have gone back in to make sure we left everything how Mikey and Ronan like it. I start my car and wait for the air to kick on. Lord knows I could use some cooling down.

I see Enzo's darken, the lights turned off, and wait for Jay to make his way back outside. After another minute the air blows cool through the vents, but I still don't see Jay. I wait a little longer until I'm sure he's not coming back out. Now I'm really confused. Why would he be in an empty pizza place in total darkness?

Saturday and Sunday come and go and no word from Jay. *Obviously, Claire.* Because you decided to throw yourself at him instead of giving him your number.

To be fair, he didn't ask for it either. Actually, he let me walk away without doing much at all. But what did I expect? Okay, so maybe I briefly thought he would show up at my parent's house to ask them where I live. Maybe look up my number in the system at Monroe's? No such luck on either account.

So, the weekend passed by, and all I had to remind me of him was my hoodie that smelled like his usual scent. Unfortunately, the cheese curl stain on my sweatshirt killed that idea, so in the washer it went. Now all that remained was my recollection of the best kiss I've ever had. Amazing. Epic. Ten out of ten would recommend.

The way his lips felt on mine. How his tongue explored my mouth. When he pinned me against the wall, placing soft kisses down my neck. I have never felt something so invigorating. I wanted all of him, right there on that checkered floor. I might be embarrassed by how bad I needed him, still need him, but judging by the way he shoved his hands into his pockets, stretching his jeans while he backed away, I think it's safe to say he felt it too.

Despite the kiss, I want to spend more time with him. Learn more about what makes him tick. The problem is, does he feel the same way about me? I was going crazy replaying the kiss in my mind and cycling through all of the ways he might be feeling about it. Surely no guy is going to turn down a good hookup, but could he want more too? I need to know. Which is why I am spending this fine Monday morning, yet again, waiting in line at Whisk! to buy a box of blondies. I'm hoping this batch isn't as cursed as the last and that the blondie gods redeem themselves with this buttery-soft offering that I plan to bring to Jay.

There are two people in front of me when I hear the bell on the door jingle, signaling someone walking in. Glancing back, I quickly divert my sight to the box of sugary goodness in front of me, avoiding all eye contact with the newest customer. Margie, mom's friend from church, whose grandson is starting at Jefferson in the fall, saunters in behind me. I hold my breath like maybe if I suffocate myself she won't be able to see me.

"Claire Dawson? Is that you?" Fail.

I slowly spin around and am faced with a five-foot-nothing old lady with floral print glasses and a short white bob.

"I thought that was you! How is your summer? Did your mother tell you my grandson will be at Jefferson next year? Ooh, Whisk!'s famous blondies, your mom and dad's favorite!"

Unsure of where to start with responding to *any* of that, I attempt to ignore all of it and keep it brief. "Hi Margie, how are you doing?"

"So, do you think my Benny will have you in class next year?" Okay, another fail.

"Oh, I'm not sure. I was telling Mom, the schedule usually doesn't come out until closer to Aug–"

Margie interrupts me. "You know, I was looking at the Jefferson website and I didn't see your picture under the faculty and staff. It was the craziest thing. A mistake I'm sure." Though, despite her *certainty*, she looks at me expecting a response.

As if the blondie gods wished to begin their redemption, the lady at the register calls for the next customer, and I see I am the only one left in line.

"So sorry, Margie, that's me. Have a great day!" I sprint to the check-out counter and greet the employee with a sigh of relief. "I owe you my firstborn," I whisper to her, handing her my card. She smiles politely, hiding the fact that she thinks I'm certifiably insane.

17

Jamison

"Try it now!" I call to Sean from behind the hood of a silver Honda Civic. The engine revs to life. I slam the hood shut and hold out my open palm waiting for Sean to exit the car. With a heavy sigh, he reaches into his pocket and pulls out a twenty, slapping it begrudgingly into my hand.

Sometimes, when the guys and I are bored, we make bets on different things at the garage. What color car will pull in next? What type of person will be driving it? How many times will Zeke fall asleep at his desk? Today, I bet Sean I could replace Mrs. Reed's alternator in under an hour. Fifty-seven minutes later, I'm twenty bucks richer.

The schedule has been light today. A dead battery here, a flat tire there, and then Mrs. Reed earning me a little extra cash. It's a nice problem to have after working so much overtime this week, but it also means more downtime to think about Claire.

The last forty-eight hours have been agonizing. To go from finally being with her to complete radio silence is a new form of torture, even for me. For the first time, maybe ever, I felt okay slightly opening up to a woman. That combined with the magic that was that fucking kiss, turned my world completely upside down.

All I have thought about the last two days is her. Like nicotine, when she hit, adrenaline coursed through my veins. But now, the withdrawal from it has left me on edge. Unsteady. Restless, until I can next satisfy the urge. The ease of conversation, the lack of judgment, the way she knew exactly what to say. Her hand in my hair, her body against mine, her tongue brushing against my own. I thought that kiss would get her out of my system. A quick high and then I'd fall back down to Earth, fulfilled. Satisfied. But it's only worse. She's the most dangerous kind of drug. I avoid this type of situation on purpose. How do I let myself get attached to someone who can just bring me pain? Who can leave? Who deserves more than me in the first place?

I walk through the bay doors for some fresh air. Leaning against the concrete wall, I slide a cigarette into place. I close my eyes still thinking of her. Sean returns from pulling the car around back and instantly leans against the wall next to me. Unfortunately for me, he also sees the benefit of a slower day and for him, it's that this is the first free moment he's gotten to confront me about Friday.

"So, what the fuck was up with Friday night?"

"Dude, don't start. That idiot in the jersey had it coming. If you had heard—"

"Not with that guy!" he cuts me off. "I don't care about the bar. You say he had it coming, he had it coming. I'm talking about the lady!"

I shake my head now confused. "What?"

"The girl you were with! At Enzo's? Come on, don't hold back on me."

I kick off the wall and face him completely. "How the hell did you find out about that?"

"Mikey texted Ro and told him you were havin' late-night snackies with a total babe, and Ro told me. Because *he's* a good friend."

I roll my eyes. "You guys seriously have got to get a life. And I didn't tell you because..." I pause, looking off to the side. "Because there's nothing to tell."

Sean brings his palm to his forehead. "Okay, I have known you for five years—"

"Three years."

"Okay, three years. But I've been your best friend—"

"Ronan's my best friend."

"Fine. *You* have been *my* best friend for three years. In those three years, you have talked about a woman exactly zero times. And now, all of a sudden, you just bring this girl to Enzo's, and your *residence* I may add, and there's nothing to tell?"

I consider all of the ways that I could respond to that, but in keeping with my newest trend, I try the truth. "The guy selling the Maverick, it's his daughter. We met when I returned the car. Ran into each other at Enzo's once before and then again on Friday. We hung out. That's all."

"Oh, you just hung out? After closing. With a good-looking girl. Whose dad owns the car of your dreams? While eating the world's best pi—"

This time, it's me who does the interrupting. "Yes, Sean. We just hung out. Now can we drop it?" I realize it's my anxiety causing me to snap. I take a long drag of my cigarette to consider everything. Talking about this makes it so much more real. What if she's already forgotten about the whole thing? See, this is why I don't do this. There's now something at stake. No, keeping our time tucked away in my memory is its safest place for now. There's a scary thought.

"Well did you at least get her number?"

Jesus, even he thinks of it. Again, I get restless. Dropping my smoke, I move my hands to my hips, hang my head, and exhale a defeated sigh.

"No. I didn't," I say angrily, and as I do, I realize I'm mad at myself, not him. Dialing it back, I lower my voice. "Can we just leave it alone?" I drop my hands and take my first step, heading back inside.

"Hey, Jay," I stop as Sean makes a poor excuse for whispering. "If it doesn't work out with the pizza girl..." he pauses, pointing behind me. "Maybe you can shoot your shot with her."

18

Claire

The short, stocky, guy that Jay's been talking to, points in my direction. When I pulled into the lot, parking off to the side so I had time to go unnoticed, I saw them already outside, both leaning against the wall. The stance he was in brought me right back to first seeing him on Friday night — foot perched, cigarette in hand. I almost left right then, but I thought him seeing me leave may somehow actually be worse than just showing up.

I realize that he could easily interpret me coming to his work not once, but twice, as completely psychotic, but I'm putting myself out there...again. Leaving it all on the table so to speak. So, after watching them talk for the last five minutes, while my brain thought of every possible outcome here, I decided there was no turning back. I definitely had this whole stalking thing reversed.

Now I'm here, standing in front of Monroe's, looking at the back of Jay's beautiful head and suffocating a white, cardboard Whisk! box with a firm grip and clammy hands. Romantic. I can hear the music from the indoor speakers playing *Tiny Dancer*, and I smile thinking back to our conversation about our favorite singers.

When he said his were these incredible legends, I was almost self-conscious. He's such an old soul, and there I was, about to admit that mine is a rock-pop singer with a pink mohawk and an attitude problem. My saving grace was that Elton John and Pink! practically dress the same so, no argument there. Plus, that girl can sing.

Suddenly, Jay whips that gorgeous body of his around, and the fact that his face instantly relaxes when he sees me is all I need. He's a man of few words, but the way his strong exterior seems to settle, tells me everything I want to know. Everything I was hoping for.

Knowing I should probably speak, I search my brain for something that says *"It's totally normal that I just showed up here!"* Reasoning, an explanation, a made-up story for all I care, but I struggle to find the best way to explain that my brain wouldn't turn off until I saw him again.

"Hi," I say. Okay, so not exactly what I was thinking, but it's a word so that's a start. He walks a pace towards me and shoves both hands in his pockets, shaking his head as if to clear his mind.

"Hi!" I hear back, only it's his friend who talks first, stepping forward and offering an energetic wave. "I'm Sean." He extends his palm to mine. Releasing a hand from the blondies, I return the gesture. "And you are..."

"Claire," Jay says quietly.

Still holding my hand he looks at Jay. "Claire?" After a brief pause his eyebrows shoot up, his eyes as wide as saucers. "Oh! Claireeeeeeee." He draws out my name. Turning back to me, hands still together, he adds, "You wouldn't happen to, oh I don't know, eat pizza?" He throws Jay a wink.

"And, that's enough." Jay grabs Sean by the shoulders and pulls our hands apart. He pushes him back towards the garage doors. "He was just leaving."

"Bye, Claireeee." Sean calls over his shoulder as he stumbles from the force of Jay's push.

I can't help but laugh, only stopping when suddenly Jay is back in front of me and his eyes are doing that piercing thing I've become so accustomed to in the last few days. This visit was much easier when it was just a thought in my mind. Seeing him here, with all of the tall, muscular, intimidating parts, is a completely different story.

"Hi," I say again and his face softens, the look he gives me, so calm I could get lost in it. For someone who often looks conflicted, he wears peace well. Relishing in it, I wait to speak.

Finally, I hold the box up to him and smile cheerfully. "I brought blondies!"

He breaks his stare and chuckles, completely thrown off guard. "You brought blondies?"

"To say thanks for taking a look at the Maverick?" It wasn't supposed to come out as a question.

He snickers again. "You brought dessert to a garage of red-blooded mechanics?"

Suddenly my cheeks flush with embarrassment. This was a terrible idea. Holding my breath I feel the creases under my arms become slick with humiliation.

He puts a hand on my shoulder, looking serious. "You may be the bravest woman I've ever met." I exhale feeling my cheeks return to their normal color and then roll my eyes playfully.

"I'm serious!" He brings his palm to his chest earnestly. "I'm high class compared to these guys. Come on." Placing his hand on my lower back he guides me inside. Thankfully my legs still work despite the sudden weakness in my knees.

Man, he wasn't kidding. These guys are animals! They all but mauled me to get the blondies, leaving only crumbs behind.

When we first walked in, Jay yelled to the garage that there was food. No literally, *"FOOD!"* was all he said and six guys, including Sean and Zeke who I already knew, came running in my direction like a herd of wild horses. Every hand that reached into the box was covered with motor oil, yet no one seemed to care. One guy even rolled out from beneath a car, had another mechanic put a blondie in his mouth, and then rolled back under. It was fascinating. Like watching animals in the zoo at feeding time.

Jay just now gets a chance to introduce me. "This is Claire. Her dad owns the Maverick."

Despite both of those things being facts, my ego is slightly bruised when he says that instead of "The devastatingly good kisser that he was falling head over heels for." Either way, the guys are all polite, saying hello through mouthfuls of blondies or at least offering a nod in my direction. One of the guys, who says his name is Rick, follows up by asking whether or not my dad has sold the car.

"Not yet," I answer. "He has a couple of people interested, but so far, it's still sitting in my parent's garage." *Much to my mother's dismay.* I fold up the empty box still blown away by what just took place and toss it into a nearby trash can.

It's funny, I assumed Dad would sell the Maverick to the first bidder just to get rid of the thing, but he's been much pickier than I expected. *"This one's just a kid," "That offer's too low."* I'm starting to think getting rid of the last thing he has of Grandpa's may be harder than he thought.

Sean smacks Jay's sculpted arm with the back of his hand. "Still got a chance, man!" Jay rolls his eyes unamused.

I subtly turn to him, but he's avoiding my gaze. Is Jay interested in the car?

We're interrupted by Zeke before I have a chance to ask. "So Jay, you bringin' Claire to Madison's 21st?"

Jay shifts uncomfortably from one foot to another. "Zeke man, I told you, nightclubs aren't really my scene."

Zeke scoffs. "Oh, and I'm a frequent flyer." He makes a gesture down his heavy frame, finishing with two pats to his very impressive beer belly.

"I'm just saying, I appreciate the invite, but I think I'm going to pass on this one."

Having known Maddie, through Zeke, since I learned to drive, I cut in. "Wait, Maddie's turning twenty-one already?" I know I'm not old, but there's something about someone whose sweet sixteen pictures you've seen, being able to drink legally, that'll make you feel ancient.

"Don't remind me." Zeke blows through his lips. "Goin' all out too. Private party at Neon Nights and everything. She invited the whole crew." Scanning the lot of guys as he speaks, he lands on Jay and holds his stare. "So damn any one of you if you let down my little girl." Jay stares back very unintimidated.

Changing the mood, another voice chimes in. "She's most excited to see me though right, boss?" This time it's Sean who gestures down *his* thick frame.

"Nobody's excited to see *that*, Sean," Wheely-Guy shouts from under the car and everybody snickers.

"So help you God if you go anywhere near her."

Sean laughs. "Good one, boss!" but Zeke's face is stone-cold.

In an attempt to save Sean's dignity, and life apparently, I cut in again. "Well, nightclubs aren't really my thing either, but I'd love to celebrate with Maddie." *And have a chance to spend more time with Jay.*

Jay snaps his head to me, his expression curious. Am I fooling anybody by pretending to be interested in Maddie's birthday? "If that's okay with you?" I add.

I feel my chest grow tight at the thought that he could completely humiliate me right here in front of everyone if he says no. *Maybe you should have thought of that first, Claire.* See, this is why it's so important that I overthink before I speak.

He nods in response, creasing his brow, which tells me he's feeling one of two things, either unexpectedly surprised or thoroughly creeped out. My wheels begin turning as I start thinking maybe I'm doing too much. I am never one to be this bold and here I am, showing up at his work and inviting myself to be his plus one all on the same day.

As if reading my mind, he adjusts his posture, his hand that was once by his side, casually grazing mine. "Sounds good to me." A subtle, yet intentional brush of his pinky seals the deal. And I feel it head to toe.

19

Jamison

I wake up in a cold sweat, my body tense and my breathing ragged. I look at the clock - 4:41 am. Less than an hour until my alarm goes off. This happens all the time, and I hate it. I wake up with time left before I have to start my day but usually can't fall back to sleep. Sometimes I grab a book from my nightstand that I've already read a thousand times. Maybe <u>The Call of the Wild</u> or <u>Of Mice and Men</u> — a story that I relate to, with hardships but no surprises because I always know how it's going to end. Today though, I decide to get a workout done instead.

Having the same nightmares on repeat, you'd think my body would get used to it by now. God knows my mind has. At this point, the dreams play like cartoons on a Saturday morning — expected and familiar — yet without fault, I snap awake almost every time.

Peeling myself from bed, I grab my pack of cigarettes. Is it completely counterproductive to smoke before I exercise? Probably. Do I care? Absolutely fucking not. Plus, it'd be worse if I smoked and didn't lift, right? So it's kind of like the two cancel each other out. Besides, after that nightmare, I could use a smoke or three.

I'm playing marbles on the floor, and Jackson is reading out loud on the bed above me. The lack of light from my window tells me it's late. Normally, I would be nervous. When I'm alone, the darkness scares me like it's supposed to when you're young. There are creepy sounds and spooky shadows, but unlike most kids who are afraid of what is hidden, I'm afraid of what is in plain sight.

Not when Jackson is here though. When he's home, I feel safe. It could be the ten-year age gap, but as long as he's around, which isn't as often as I would like, I'm not worried about what comes home — Jackson will protect me. If there is fighting or yelling, he will sit with me in the closet, both of us scrunched up to fit against the back wall.

Sometimes we sit in silence, sometimes we talk. Sometimes he shows me how to hold a cigarette, me pretending with a broken crayon or rolled up piece of paper, him with the real thing. Either way, he almost always ends up reading to me until Mom comes to get us. <u>The Adventures of Huckleberry Finn</u> is my favorite. We must have read that book a hundred times already. It's the one he's reading now.

"Well, it made me sick to see it; and I was sorry for them poor pitiful rascals, it seemed like I couldn't ever feel any hardness against them any more in the world. It was a dreadful thing to see. Human beings can be awful cruel to one another." Jackson stops reading.

"It's true, Jay," he says, still lying at the bottom of the bed so he can see me on the floor. "People in this world can be real dickheads. These losers Mom brings home, can all go to Hell. But you know, not everyone out there sucks so bad. We just have to get out of this fucking place."

I shoot my head up to him, rolling marbles in my palm. "You mean, like leave?" Looking down, I watch the colorful beads move freely in my hand. "I don't know, Jack. I don't think Mom would ever leave this place."

"Not Mom, Jay — you. Mom's made her mess, but you have to promise me you'll leave one day. Get out of his house, and make a life for yourself. Just run, Jay, like Huck did. When you're big enough, okay?"

The idea of leaving scares me. The idea of running away and being on my own. And does he mean I should leave Mom behind? "Big like you, Jack?" I ask.

"Yeah, buddy." He hides his face behind the book, but I hear the way his voice changes. "Big like me."

Jackson stayed up all night finishing the book one last time for me. When I woke up in the morning, still on the floor below his bed, he was gone.

Claire showed up at Monroe's. I still can't believe it. I know she said she was there as a thank you from her dad, but I'm hoping at least a small part of her was happy for the chance to see me. I know I was really fucking happy that I got to see her.

Not only did she come to work with the best goddamn dessert I've ever had, but she also agreed to go to Maddie's party with me. At least I think she meant with me. I panicked a little when she said she'd love to go, so I'm not sure where we landed in terms of plans. That's what I'm trying to find out now. If I would just stop being such a pussy and text her already.

I finally asked Claire for her number before she left the garage. By some twisted turn of events, Zeke wingmanned for me by throwing this stupid party and gave me an excuse to need it. At that point, I was running a little on autopilot from all of the surprises, so thankfully, I didn't have enough brain power to worry about how it looked.

"I'll text you about the party then I guess?" She let out an adorable giggle, and I caught myself noticing things like fucking adorable giggles. Writing her number on the back of a Monroe's business card, she handed it to me.

"I guess we'll see."

Now I am sitting at Enzo's, with my phone and the card with a little heart next to the last number, contemplating life and my first text to her.

"Holy shit, dude, just send it already." Ronan and I are at an empty table as he folds pizza boxes after closing, and I completely lose my dignity. A new message screen is pulled up with Claire's name at the top. My finger hovers over the little blue arrow that will send the text and seal my fate.

After going back and forth about what to say way too many times, I landed on the facts.

ME: Hey, it's Jay. Party is at Neon Nights on Friday at 9. Cool?

As I hesitate a minute longer, Ronan stops midfold. "What is with you, man? I have never seen you give a single fuck about what you text someone."

It's true. I rarely text at all and when I do, they're almost always to Ro, Mikey, or Sean and usually consist of one-word responses or the middle finger emoji. Never in my life have I mulled over whether or not to say "Hey." or "What's up?" or to add a smiley face or exclamation point to the end of a message.

"I don't know, Ro. I thought I was messed up before." I drop my head in my hands, elbows on the table. "But my head is so fucked right now."

"You actually like this girl, don't you?"

I lift my head and look at him. The question is rhetorical. My actions say it all, but I know what Ronan means. If anyone knows that I don't form true connections, it's him. His big personality is the reason we even became real friends. Yeah, we had the quiet bond of two foster kids living in the same hell hole, but he's the one who reached out after he left the house. And he never quit.

No matter where I went, he somehow got a hold of me. He was relentless and intentional, and I have him and him alone to thank for our friendship. Eventually, it balanced out, once I knew he was sticking around, but he took on most of the load in the beginning. He would never say it outright but that's what he means now. He knows that the fact that I'm even making the first move is huge. Even if it is over some dumb party.

Taking one final deep breath, I hit send on my phone and flip it over. Is this what it feels like to care what someone thinks? I knew there was a reason I never did this type of thing.

Ronan laughs and puts a finished box to the side. With a smile on his face, he folds one more. I'm not sure if he's talking about the text I'm sending or the risk he knows I'm taking, but flipping the lid he says, "Bout fucking time."

20

Claire

I leap for my phone on my bedside table, nearly throwing my computer from my lap. I gave Jay my number at Monroe's and have been waiting for him to use it ever since. I even kept my phone on loud during my tutoring sessions, and I haven't done that since the Spring Break incident of last year.

The week we had off, Chloe went to Cabo with her then-boyfriend, Connor. He was older than her and completely loaded. After just two weeks together he surprised her with a trip to an all-inclusive on the coast. She was gone from Monday to Saturday and afterward, came right to my house from the airport to give me all the details.

The details turned out to be a half hour of her filling me in on all of the wild places they banged, most of which I can't unhear. After a repulsive thirty minutes, she went home, and I left for the library. I was only halfway through my tutoring session when The Lonely Island's *I Just Had Sex*, started playing from my phone on full volume. Apparently, Chloe thought it would be funny to change my ringtone without letting me know and introduce little Johnny to one biology lesson I wasn't prepared to teach.

Karma got Chloe back though just three days later, when she got a call from the resort saying that Mr. Seth Landon's credit card had bounced for their room. Turns out Connor was not so loaded after all. He was also not only unemployed and living in his mother's basement, but he was a criminal who frequently committed credit card fraud. After that, I called us even.

So here we are, over forty-eight hours after giving Jay my number and a full year from the last time I had my volume on loud, and my phone finally dings with a message from him.

JAY: Hey, it's Jay. Party is at Neon Nights on Friday at 9. Cool?

Okay so not a complete confession of love but it's more than three words so I'll take it.

ME: Sounds good to me. Do we want to meet there?

I hit send before I have a chance to edit it a hundred times. I mean, it's a ride — does it really matter how he answers? But as soon as it's delivered, I realize which way I want him to respond. It's like when you toss a coin into the air and as soon as it's out of your hand, you've already chosen a side you hope it lands on.

JAY: I can grab you on my way if you want.

Heads it is.

ME: Perfect.

Realizing he's only ever been to my parent's house, I send my address too.

The three bubbles appear showing that he's typing and then disappear again. I wait for him to respond — to text back anything to keep the conversation going. But he's a man of few words and after enough time has passed that I know our exchange has come to an end, I silence my phone, put it back on my nightstand next to my laptop, and hit the light.

As I snuggle under the covers, I think about the collection of conversations that I've had with Jay over the last week. I realize that I don't mind that he isn't the chattiest of guys. With him, he says what he means and he means what he says. There's no fake chit-chat, no sugarcoating things. His words are like shooting stars — rare and fleeting but if you're lucky, you just might catch a glimpse.

"I like classic cars. And you."

I roll over and grab my phone to send a text of my own. There's a notification for one new message already waiting.

JAY: See you then, Claire.

Smiling, I close out our chain to type out the text I planned on sending.

ME: Be here tomorrow to shop for a new outfit. Guess who finally has plans Friday night.

Almost immediately I get a response.

CHLOE: IT'S HAPPENING!

I send a thumbs-up emoji as another text comes in.

CHLOE: Jay boy wants to rev your engine, doesn't he?

Then another.

CHLOE: Tap your bumper?

And another.

CHLOE: Flick your headlights?

Laughing to myself, I set my phone down again and roll back into bed.

I drift off to sleep humming the tune to *I just had sex* and thinking of shooting stars.

I get back from my run to see Chloe sitting on the steps to my apartment with two coffees from Busy's in her hand. I feel bad that she's starting to sweat from the morning sun, but to be fair, when I said I wanted her here to go shopping, I thought she'd come when the stores were actually open. I should have known better.

Chloe and I treat our summers very differently. Where I like to keep routine, she is very much *go with the flow.* Sometimes the flow means sleeping in until 10 am and sometimes it's hitting hot yoga before the sun comes up. Today, the flow led right to my apartment door when she realized I have a date (are we calling it that?) and she is lacking details.

She hands me my iced butterscotch latte, slurping up the last sip of her mocha cold brew.

"Were you waiting that long?" I ask, signaling to her empty drink.

"Nah, I was just super thirsty. You're lucky you got here in time. Yours was next."

Fake gasping, I pull my drink back. "Never!" I take a long sip of my latte and close my eyes in bliss. "These truly are the best."

"I know I am. Now tell me everything."

I fill her in as we walk into my building and to my apartment. Starting at the beginning I tell her all of it, from pizza at Enzo's to our text chain last night. She listens intently, nodding here, gasping there, and asking for step-by-step details of our kiss including sound effects and role play.

When she finally sets me free from my story, I leave her in my bedroom and step into the shower. From the bathroom, I hear her yell.

"So let me get this straight. You get this mysterious, *sexy* mechanic if I may add, to feed you, openly admit to liking you, and kiss you up against the wall like the intro to an adult movie?"

"Okay, I wouldn't take it that far."

"And now you are going to Neon Nights with him and a bunch of his hot, greasy friends?"

"I never said his friends were hot or greasy so I'm not sure..."

"And you're just telling me about it now!"

"I'm sorry! It all happened so fast."

I hear her scoff, and I can picture her eyes rolling as clearly as her being in here with me. "Yeah, yeah, yeah, you're forgiven. But I better receive regular updates from here on out."

Laughing from the shower I stick my head out of the curtain. The view from the bathroom leads right through the door to her sitting on my bed. Her grumpy expression would look right at home on a toddler who hadn't been allowed ice cream for dinner.

"You will be the first to know if there is anything else to tell, okay?"

"Fine," she fake sulks.

I go to pull my head back into the shower as she starts again.

"Hey, Claire..."

I look at her, waiting for her to finish.

"Sorry for interrupting your pizza porno the other night." She breaks into laughter as I pull my head back and snap the curtain shut.

"Ass!"

Once I'm dressed and ready to go, I check the time. Stores should just be opening up. We devise a plan of attack for finding the perfect outfit and both decide that hitting the mall will probably give us the most bang for our buck. So, we're off to the Center Springs mall to score a knockout dress and an Auntie Anne's pretzel.

Honestly, I'm not sure which I'm most excited about.

21

Jamison

"**D**ude, why are we here?" I walk reluctantly next to Ronan, my eyes wandering to the rows of stores on either side of us.

"Because you have your first official date with Claire tomorrow, and I'll be damned if you wear work boots and your "going out t-shirt" to a fucking nightclub," Ronan answers.

He had Mikey open the restaurant today when he heard about the party. Being that Zeke also warned me about wearing my work boots to Neon Nights, he was okay with me taking the morning to hit the mall — something I thought I would never do.

"I just can't believe I let you take me *shopping*."

Another way Ronan and I are total opposites. When I was younger, I got used to having a few shirts and a pair of shoes to my name, and once I started making my own money, I didn't feel the need to broaden my wardrobe. Ro, who used to not care at all about his appearance, was the opposite. He used clothes as a way to give the middle finger to everything that happened so to speak, and take on a new identity. Now, you'd never know it, but hidden beneath his apron are Levi's in all different shades. And on the rare occasion that he isn't throwing pizzas, he's usually sporting crisp new crewneck tees and clean high-top Converse.

On the other hand, being that I go out like once a month, I can usually get by with a black t-shirt and one of my two pairs of jeans — which was my plan for tomorrow — until Ro found out. Now he is adamant that the occasion calls for something better.

"It's a party, man. At a club. You need something you haven't owned since *your* twenty-first, and I need to know my best friend is lookin' his best."

He's probably right. I haven't been anywhere worth dressing up for in a very long time. Let alone with a girl I wouldn't hate to impress.

"Alright, first stop." We're standing outside of the Vans store. "I know you're not a Converse guy, so this is a close second." They're practically the same thing, but as I look around, he's kinda right. Despite being very similar, I think I can get on board with Vans a little more.

I pick out a pair of black low tops with a matching black sole, much like the one I wear on the inside. Near the register, I see a shirt I don't particularly hate. Okay, so it is a black t-shirt but unlike my usual, there is a pocket in the upper left corner with their slogan *Off The Wall* written in teal. Adding it to my shoes, I kill two birds with one stone. I show Ro the shirt as we exit the store.

"Alright, so more like a pivot than a complete one-eighty, but not bad. Now, jeans."

He is multiple strides away from me when he realizes I've stopped walking with him. He turns back and gives me a *what-the-hell* look, but my legs have stopped working because I'm staring at Claire. At this point I should just expect to see her everywhere I go — even outside of Maple Grove apparently. Did this happen before we met too? Is it possible that we've been in the same place even before this week?

Ronan looks toward my view and then raises his brows at me. Sucking my teeth, I nod as if to say, *"Yep. That's her,"* and he closes the gap between us.

"Which one?"

Claire and the same girl that she first came to Monroe's with, are standing in line for Auntie Anne's pretzels. Both girls are holding several bags from stores I've never even heard of. Claire is wearing a pair of cut-off shorts and a tank top, reminiscent of the first day we met. Her friend is in bike shorts and an oversized graphic tee that I can't quite see from here. The blonde must say something funny because Claire throws her head back laughing, and I'm immediately jealous that I wasn't the one who caused that reaction. Her hair hangs in waves behind her, her perfect chin pointing to the ceiling. Even from here, I can see her long dark lashes, and the carefree way she holds herself, once again, puts me at ease.

"Tall brunette."

Ro lets out a deep breath. "Oh, thank God."

I'm confused by his response until I turn to see him staring a hole through Claire's friend. Now I'm the one throwing my head back. I'm also curious what he would have done if I had said Claire was the petite blonde one.

Suddenly, like two opposite poles of a magnet are drawn to each other, even from afar, she looks in my direction. Her mouth drops open in surprise, then much like mine, shifts as if it should be expected.

I smack Ro's chest with the back of my hand to let him know we're moving. Together we walk towards Claire and her friend who are next in line.

"Hi," I say, mimicking her greeting at Monroe's.

She gives a knowing smile, and I blush. I fucking blush. Making Claire happy has quickly become my new favorite thing, and she makes it so easy to do.

Her friend clears her throat dramatically. Ronan attempts to hide his amusement and Claire fakes a scoff.

"Guys, this is Chloe. Chloe, this is Jay."

"Hi again," I say, and I can now see that her shirt says, **I Can't Even** across the front.

Claire gestures to Ro, "And this is..."

"Ronan." He sticks his hand out directly to Chloe. Smooth Ro. Claire tries to hide her smile. Chloe does not.

After dropping hands, she cries, "Wait! I recognize you! From Enzo's!"

Ronan nods his head looking at me like he's impressed. "He owns the place," I say, hyping my boy up.

"What? Stop it. I LOVE your balls." Ronan all but drops to the floor.

"Oh my God! Your meatballs! She means she loves your meatball subs!" Claire smacks Chloe's arm.

"Hmm, *is* that what I mean?" Chloe says with a flirty smile. She's kidding, but I think Ronan just fell in love.

"I hate to interrupt whatever is happening here, but I think you guys are up." I cut in, pointing to the lady behind the counter of Auntie Anne's who looks like she very much hates her job.

Claire steps up and orders two cinnamon sugar pretzels and then turns back to us. "Do you guys want anything?"

"Nah, I'm good. I've never even had one of these things before," I say, looking at Ro who shrugs his shoulders and shakes his head in agreement.

Claire and Chloe's faces mirror each other, both mouths dropped open. "Make it four," Claire says immediately.

"Seriously guys," Chloe speaks up. "You haven't lived until you've tasted this sugary slice of heaven."

Both girls reach for their wallets, but I hand Ms. Sunshine my card instead.

Chloe makes a dramatic gasp. "Wow. And they say chivalry is dead." She takes the oily bag of pretzels and walks to the closest bench.

"Thanks for the food, Mr. Gentleman...again," Claire says as she follows behind Ronan. "Do you know this owner too?"

"Who? Ms. Anne? Oh sure, we go way back," I joke.

She scrunches her face and squeezes my arm, and I'm reminded all over again of the effect her touch has on me. Even now, this casual contact lights a fire deep inside.

We get to the bench and the girls sit with us standing in front of them. Chloe distributes the pretzels, and Ronan and I take our first bites. Man, they weren't kidding. These things are delicious — deep fried dough, brushed with melted butter, and drenched in cinnamon sugar? I mean, I guess I should have seen that coming, but we look at each other like we never would have guessed. Claire sure knows her sweets.

After a few moments of gluttonous silence, Chloe asks Ronan how he makes his meatballs. They start talking about the "secret ingredient," which isn't so secret (ricotta cheese), when I tune them out and turn to Claire.

"Any chance you're also here buying an outfit for Friday?" I hold up the bag in my hand internally cursing myself for bringing it up.

She mimics the gesture and my inner voice quiets. "Guilty."

We both roll our eyes, but inside I'm glad to know that she also felt the pressure to impress. My gladness though, doesn't feel like relief. It hits me out of nowhere that this isn't supposed to be happening. I'm not supposed to be happy I ran into her. Hell, I'm not supposed to be happy at all. I shouldn't be looking forward to hanging out tomorrow, and I'm damn sure not supposed to be falling for her like I am. I get lost inside my head thinking of all of the reasons I should cancel our plans, and end this before we're both in too deep, when I see her face light up. It drops again almost immediately after I don't mirror her excitement.

"Wait, what?" I regain my focus and try to catch up on what I missed.

"Oh, uh, no." She brushes her hair behind her ear. "I just said it should be a good time."

I'm an idiot. And I can't keep going back and forth like this inside my mind. It's time to decide if I'm doing this or not. If I want to get to know Claire then I have to commit to getting out of my head. It's not fair to her and it's driving me fucking crazy.

"Definitely," I say, making my decision.

She looks back up and meets my gaze. I either saved it somehow or she already understands the way I self-sabotage.

Ronan taps me on the shoulder. "Come on, Jay! We aren't finished here yet." It's honestly the perfect time, but he is way too chipper just for jean shopping. "It was nice to finally meet you, Claire," he adds.

"I guess that's my cue," I say. She stands and I give her a hug with my one free arm. "I'll see you tomorrow then." I breathe in her scent before pulling away.

"If not before." She winks but considering how the universe seems to keep putting us together, she may not be kidding. "Nice to meet you, Ronan!"

Walking away, Ro starts babbling about Chloe. She's this, she's that, wasn't it hilarious when...But I'm only half listening. Deciding I want Claire is fucking terrifying. Especially when I consider she may not want me back.

Interested? Sure.

But could she actually want all of me?

"Dude, I think that girl's my soulmate," he says.

I look back and see the girls standing to leave. Claire gives me a small wave before heading in the opposite direction.

Me too, I think. *Me too*.

22

Claire

I count the number of times the cursor on my screen blinks — one, two, three, four — as I space out, mentally running through my previous search. Earlier I decided to Google: **What jobs can you get with a teaching degree?**

I thought it might ease my anxiety about telling my parents, and planning the rest of my life, if I at least had a plan. So before our weekly dinner, I did some research. Google produced the following ideas:

Classroom teacher - Shocker.
School counselor - Unqualified.
Social worker - Too sad.
Psychotherapist - Sounds scary.
Event planner - Feels like a stretch.
Tutor - Check.
Writer - I wish.

Then there were the ones that at first glance seemed like they may actually work:

Librarian
Advisor
Curriculum planner
Instructional coach
Human Resources

After looking over the list again, I crossed off curriculum planner because honestly, that sounds like the most boring thing on the planet and then also deleted human resources. There is no way I could hire or fire anyone without wildly overthinking how to do it or whether or not they'd be mad at me afterward.

Once the list was narrowed down to three, I typed my prospects into every job search website I could find. Unfortunately, there are currently no listings under any of those categories within thirty miles. So, now I'm back to square one.

I stare at my document entitled **Novel Ideas**. I thought it was fitting in both senses of the word. I was on a roll the other night, but either my head is somewhere else now, thinking of a world full of rejection letters and unemployment, or those few bullet points were all I was capable of. I actually find myself hoping it's the first one. At least in that world, my dream isn't in the gutter. Just everything else is.

My phone dings unexpectedly, and I ready myself for Chloe's latest update.

Ever since meeting Ronan and finding out that he is Irish and not Italian, she has been down a rabbit hole of famous Irishmen.

Her last text came through about twenty minutes ago and read:

CHLOE: Did we know Bono was Irish?

To which I responded:

ME: I guess WE didn't, but I did, yes.

She then sent:

CHLOE: Okay, but did we know his real name is Paul David Hewson?

Now that I didn't know.

ME: Nope. But I'm sticking with Bono. Way more rock n' roll.

Turning my phone over, I see it's not Chloe who texted. It's Jay.

JAY: Are you hungry?

Does he even realize the way that this question is like foreplay for women?

ME: The answer is almost always yes, even if it's not.

ME: But right now I am starving.

Dinner with my parents tonight was mom's meatloaf. Between that and constantly dodging the topic of work, I barely ate a thing.

JAY: Pizza? Ro and Mikey just closed up and gave me a whole pie of leftovers.

My stomach growls at just the thought.

ME: I can be at Enzo's in 20?

I flip my laptop closed and look around for my wallet.

JAY: Actually, I thought maybe I'd bring it to you.

Wait, what? Like to my apartment?

JAY: And before you pull the stalker card, you gave me your address last night.

I laugh out loud and for half a second I wonder if this is a booty call. I mean sure, Jay seems shy and sweet, but it is almost 10 pm and he is, well...a guy. Add that he's smoking hot and I wouldn't say it's completely out of the question. I decide that in this situation, my stomach beats my mind by a mile. Besides, would it be so bad if it *was* a booty call? *Chill, Claire, damn.*

ME: Doesn't explain the mall...

ME: But sure. I'll meet you outside.

I look around at the state of my apartment. Thankfully my afternoon tutoring session was canceled today, and I spent the time panic-cleaning about work before I decided to do my Google dive. Throwing my running clothes from earlier into the hamper and putting the blender in the dishwasher from my post-mall smoothie, I decide it's pretty much as good as it's going to get.

JAY: Be there in ten.

Perfect. I spend the first four minutes attempting to find something to change into that says both *"Let's eat pizza"* and *"Please undress me"* — just in case. I land on baby pink pajama shorts with mint green polka dots and a matching lace tank. I leave on the nude cotton bra and underwear I'm wearing because if my gut is right and this is just food, sexy lingerie is going to send entirely the wrong message.

The next three minutes I spend reapplying deodorant and my vanilla body spray and practically power washing my teeth. By the time I'm done freshening up, I get outside right as Jay steps out from his truck, pizza box in hand.

He's wearing a gray t-shirt that says Monroe's Motors in navy across his perfect chest and another faded pair of jeans. He's swapped his work boots for a pair of black Vans and although they look good, I can't help but notice that I kind of miss his usual style. His hair looks freshly cut and as he approaches, I smell his familiar scent, this time mixed with dough and mozzarella cheese. He smiles without showing his teeth but his eyes tell me he's happy to be here — just one subtle gesture that I'm learning from a man who doesn't say too much out loud.

"Wow." He looks me up and down. "You look…"

"Ready for bed?" I mean it critically but his face flushes and he tightens his jaw.

"Something like that."

Now my face grows warm. The attraction between us is clearly there. That was evident from the night at Enzo's. But the lack of drawstring in his pants tells me he isn't just here for sex. Besides, would it even be a booty call if he brings me dinner first?

I stop overanalyzing and point over my shoulder. "Shall we?"

He looks me up and down again. "Let's do it."

The spot way below my belly button flips. *Not "IT" you perv.* I rip my mind from the gutter and lead him in.

When we get into my apartment, he looks around. Starting at the kitchen, he drops the pizza on the counter and then runs his hand across the small island. Next, he scans the living room, passing my couch and loveseat, touching a pillow on each as he goes. He peeks into the hallway bathroom and finally stops at my bedroom door. He sees the bed and then the connected door that leads to the full bath. His eyes are wide as he turns back to me leaning against the doorway.

"Claire, your apartment is huge."

"Is it? It kind of feels a little tight if I have people over, but it does the job." He laughs but his face says he's a million miles away.

"This isn't tight. Trust me." I wish I knew where he went when he got like this.

"Well, thanks." I smile and shrug my shoulders, not really sure what else to say.

"I live behind Enzo's." He's standing up now with both hands shoved in his pockets. I'm taken aback by how random his confession is but I try to just go with it.

"Oh, okay. I mean, that makes sense since I've seen you there more than once."

"No, Claire, not like in a complex behind the building. I live *in* Enzo's. There's an old utility closet that Ronan turned into a studio apartment if you can even call it that. And I live there. Like, behind the kitchen."

My eyes squint as I take in what he says. After I've processed, the change in his demeanor makes much more sense. He's here in my very decent apartment with one and a half bathrooms, two couches, and a queen-size bed, and he lives in a pizza shop owned by his best friend. By his body language alone, I can tell he was embarrassed to say it but my complaining about the size of my place didn't help I'm sure.

I think about how to respond. From what I can tell, Jay isn't looking for sympathy. In fact, he seems like the type who would hate it more than anything, but what am I supposed to say? *"I'm happy for you and your glorified closet?"* Where he lives doesn't matter to me but it's obviously a big deal to him.

I fix my face and take my foot out of my mouth, placing it back on the floor where it belongs. Walking over to him, I pull both of his arms from his pockets and take his hands in mine. I take a deep breath in and let it out slowly as he waits expectedly for my response.

"Jay." I pause for effect. "It won't matter where you live if I die of starvation before I ever get to see it."

He laughs, his mouth spreading into the biggest smile, before dropping his forehead to mine. We stand like that as he closes his eyes and lets out one last chuckle. I feel his shoulders relax and give his hands a small squeeze.

"Okay, fine," he says as he stands up straight, maybe a little straighter than before. "Let's eat."

23

Jamison

I flip open the pizza box, and Claire practically drools when she sees what's inside. There are a few miscellaneous slices left over from today's pies, and about half a Hawaiian that Mikey kept to the side for me when I texted him earlier tonight.

ME: Need a favor.

MIKEY: Fresh out of those.

ME: Funny. I need a pie after closing but at least a few have to be Hawaiian.

MIKEY: Done. Just took one out. I'll set some aside for you.

ME: Thanks, man.

MIKEY: This for the girl from the other night?

ME: How in the hell?

MIKEY: Ro said you got it bad.

ME: Do you two have to tell each other everything?

MIKEY: Just the good stuff.

Unreal. Apparently, my business is *everyone's* business. But Ronan's not wrong. I do have it bad.

After the mall this morning, I knew I couldn't wait until tomorrow to see Claire. My run-ins with her around town have been the highlight of my week — hell of my last six months. And I just wanted another chance to be with her. Tomorrow will be cool, being out with her for the first time, but we'll be surrounded by strangers in a dark club with loud music. Tonight I just want her all to myself.

Having seen her eat Enzo's the first time, I knew she wouldn't pass it up. So, at the risk of looking like a total fucking creep, I decided texting her this late was worth a shot. Would I hate pressing her against another wall and kissing my way down her body? No. But did I come here just for that? Also, no.

I came because I like talking to her, and I can't get her out of my fucking head. This girl is like two ends of a spectrum. Like the first drag of a cigarette after a long, shitty day — she's soothing but intoxicating. When I'm around her my body relaxes but my heart starts to race. When I'm not, there's that withdrawal again. So here I am, acting totally out of character — quenching my most recent thirst.

Claire carries the pizza box to the coffee table and pats the spot on the couch next to her.

"Do you want to tell me where the plates are?"

She's already mid-cheesepull when she mumbles out, "Don't bother." I watch her wrap the cheese around her tongue until it finally separates from itself. God, this girl's amazing.

Sitting next to her, I grab a piece of plain for myself. I don't mind Hawaiian but she looks like she's about to put it back, so I'll save those for her.

"So wuh you bah at tha mall?" Her cheeks are already full as she pops a piece of pineapple into her mouth that first went rogue onto her lap.

"I'm sorry, what?"

She chews her bite dramatically, swallows, and then licks her lips. She's not trying to be sexy but goddamn if it isn't the most seductive thing I've ever seen.

"What did you buy at the mall?" She takes another bite waiting for my answer.

"Jeans, a t-shirt, and these." I put one foot on the coffee table next to the box. I realize I now have my dirty shoe on her table next to our food and quickly pull it back.

"I like them," she says as she stands up. She comes back with a roll of paper towels and two beers. Handing one to me, she opens the other and takes a long sip. "But just when I was getting used to the boots."

I wouldn't have pinned her as a beer girl, but I'm not complaining. I crack mine open and take a sip before sitting it on the lid of the box. Somewhere deep in my chest, I feel a warmth spread to a very buried place, and it's not from the alcohol. It's a pair of shoes but it's like her telling me she doesn't mind the boots, is her telling me she's accepting me for who I am. *That's because she doesn't know the rest,* I think.

"Oh, don't worry, they aren't going anywhere."

She smiles and grabs another slice.

"So you never told me what you do. You know where I work." I change subjects and shove the self-deprecating thought back down. *Not all at once,* I respond to myself. A reminder that I am opening up little by little. It's easy to feel like I'm hiding all of my demons but I realize I don't know much about her either. I guess this is how it starts.

"Well, for the last three years, I taught middle school English." She sets her slice back in the box and pulls a pillow to her lap. "But they cut my position at the end of last school year. Budget cuts meant combining classes and combining classes meant needing fewer teachers. Unfortunately for me, the other English teacher had been there for almost a decade so," she raises her hand, "short end of the stick."

"Shit, that sucks. They can't just move you somewhere else?"

"There's no need anywhere else in the district right now, and honestly," she picks up her can, "I'm not sure I would have accepted another spot anyway."

"Why's that?"

She fidgets in her seat, pulling her legs up and then putting them back down. Finally, she settles with one on the floor and one beneath her, tucked under the other.

"I kind of started to hate my job." She takes a sip. "I know it's cliché and probably kind of entitled to say, but I just think I'm too young to be spending my life doing something I don't even like."

I consider this a minute. She's not wrong. It's not pretty, and I don't make a fortune, hell I even complain about it, but at the end of the day, I love what I do. I love fixing cars and helping people appreciate them again. I spent more than the first half of my existence living a life I hated. I don't think I could do it again. Especially, if I had a say in the matter this time.

"And what do you like?"

She sets her can down and wraps her arms around the pillow.

"I like to write." I nod, remembering our conversation about hobbies, as she loses herself in thought for just a second. Reaching for her beer, she snaps back into focus. "I'd actually like to do that for real, but as my dad would say, writing doesn't pay the bills, so..."

"I used to steal cars when I was younger."

She chokes on the sip she just took and places her can back on the table. "Okay, so we're spilling all of our secrets. Got it." She's kidding but all I can think is, *you don't know the half of it*.

"Not my best moment, I know. But I would hot-wire cars I could tell needed work and then fix them up behind an abandoned warehouse." I pause to take a sip of my beer.

"Wait, you would steal cars, just to work on them?"

"Yep. Sometimes I'd be in a tight spot and had to sell them," *for food or cigarettes or money for rent*, "but most of the time I would just leave them somewhere I knew they'd be found."

She's looking at me intensely. I can't tell what she's thinking, but the fact that her reaction isn't instant judgment or disgust encourages me to keep going.

"I was fifteen and in foster care. I couldn't hold a job because I was always moving, and I couldn't afford my own car because I didn't have any money. But cars made me happy, still do, and all I wanted to do was get my hands in them." I wish I could blame the alcohol for putting all of this out there, but I'm not even halfway done my damn beer.

"I guess my point is, that doing something you love doesn't always have to pay the bills too. Sometimes you can do something just because it makes you happy." It doesn't seem like a hard concept to grasp but nowadays everything comes back to making money. But, having come from a place where I lost everything except for my passion, I know how priceless it can be to just hold onto something you love.

Claire smiles with her eyes. I love that her face isn't full of pity. If anything, it looks like…pride? There are a lot of feelings I have around everything in my past — regret, anger, shame, hate — but feeling sorry for myself, isn't one of them, and Claire seems to get that. She just seems to get everything about me. *Everything she knows.*

Claire extends her hand across the couch. I set my can down, place my palm on hers and our fingers intertwine. Two perfect interlocking pieces.

"Thanks for that," is all she says.

I brush my thumb along hers and she sucks in a slow breath. Between the sound she makes, her smooth skin, and our raw communication, I suddenly need her close to me.

I tug her arm gently, pulling her to me. She crawls across the couch until her knees touch my hip. Still, it isn't close enough.

I grab her by the waist and guide her to my lap, slowly releasing her so she's straddling my legs. I'm instantly hard and by the way she sits deeper onto me, I know she can feel it under my jeans. I reach up and tuck a stray wave behind her ear so I can see her whole face. Her eyelids hang heavy and that mouth I've fantasized about for days sits right in front of me — lips parted, panting, asking to be kissed. When she bites her lip, I fucking lose it.

Grabbing her face with both hands, I pull her in and kiss her like I've wanted to since the first time it happened. Our tongues brush, and Claire whimpers the most delicious sound. It feels eager and greedy. Like we've been deprived of each other for too long. And we have been.

She wraps her arms around my neck and pulls our bodies closer as if any space between us is too much. I drag my fingertips down her back and she arches it in response. Skimming the exposed skin above the waistband of her shorts, she grinds her hips under my touch, and I pull them down harder to increase the pressure.

Claire removes her arms from around my neck and glides her hands along the bottom of my shirt. She pulls it over my head and throws it to the ground in one fell swoop. I catch her taking in all of me as she runs her fingers over the rise and fall of several scars. She leans forward and kisses the one below my collarbone. A rough circle where Foster Dad number five decided to use me as an ashtray because I stepped in front of the TV. Her kiss is so soft and gentle, so delicate in contrast to the burn she places it on — to what we're feeling now.

I reach up and gather her hair to one shoulder. I wrap it around my fist like I've thought about so many times before and gently pull it so the other side of her neck is completely exposed. I kiss behind her ear and then again, lower, and lower, until I reach the lace of her shirt, stopping at the same spot she did on me.

Her flawless chest heaves under my lips and I suck, leaving my mark on her in the same location. Claire hums, her cleavage vibrating beneath my touch. I move my hand to one curve, grazing my thumb across the middle, taking everything in me not to completely fucking bury myself between the two.

Catching me by surprise, she grabs my wrist and pulls it away.

For a second, I think I did something wrong — that she wants me to stop. That is until she places one foot on the ground and then the other, pulling me up with her. I instantly miss the weight of her on me. I want to beg for the pressure back, but she turns towards her bedroom, and I follow her instead.

This is not what I came here for. I mean, of course I want her, need her even, but the last thing I want, is for her to think I came here for a booty call. She, I hope, is becoming so much more than that.

Claire sits back on the bed and reaches for the hem of her shirt. Pulling it over her head, I wince at how beautiful she is. She is making what I'm about to do so much harder.

"Claire." I step forward, leaving space between us.

"Jay." She grabs my belt loops and closes the gap.

Rubbing the back of my neck, I close my eyes and muster up all of the self-control I have.

"I'm not going to do this."

She freezes where she is, before dropping her face. Her hands follow suit.

I put her chin between my fingers and tilt it to me.

"It's not that I don't want to. Because trust me," I look down at where my pants bulge from the strain underneath, "I really fucking want to. But I don't want any part of you to think this was my plan." I move a loose hair back into place. "I came here because I wanted to be with you, Claire. All of you. Not just like this." She exhales and then looks at me understandingly.

"I get it," she says. "This wasn't my plan either."

I drop to the floor, kneeling between her legs. I run my hands up her thighs and let out a heavy sigh, cursing myself for doing what I know is right. I pull her head to mine and kiss her hard one more time. She leans into the kiss hungry for more. Breaking apart reluctantly, I rest my forehead on hers.

"I'll see you tomorrow."

She smiles. "See you tomorrow."

I stand, looking down at her one more time. I trace the outline of her lips with my thumb. I can't believe I'm here.

And I can't believe I'm leaving.

"You're fucking flawless."

Before I can see her reaction, I walk straight for my shirt and out of her apartment, knowing if I hesitate for even a second, I might change my mind.

24

Claire

That cold shower did absolutely nothing to cool me off. Standing under the running water, my mind kept racing back to just moments before. It took me a solid ten minutes to even move from my bed once I heard the door close behind him. I wasn't sure if I was upset or impressed that Jay decided to leave after I sprawled half my naked body before him. In the end, I think I landed on a combination of both — upset not because he hurt my feelings but because I was disappointed he wouldn't stay. Impressed because his self-control was incredible.

Feeling how much of him wanted me, knowing how much of me wanted him back — how no amount of friction was enough. His hands in my hair, on my back, both of us wanting more. Walking out that door took a type of discipline I just don't possess.

I saw a lot of Jay tonight that was new to me. Parts of his past, parts of his body — the scars on both the inside and the outside that marked areas I had never seen before. And despite him sharing more of himself in both ways, there's so much to him that I still don't know. For a guy so seemingly simple, he's the most complex person I've ever met. An alcoholic mother, abuse, foster care? I mean the man stole cars just to make himself happy. It's like he's slowly peeling away the layers that seem to protect him from the world, but they're like pieces of a puzzle I have yet to fit together. It would be nice if the final picture would reveal itself to me all at once instead of little by little but for now, I'll take what I can get.

I saw a lot of myself tonight too, which was also entirely new to me. Who knew I was capable of taking charge and that when I did, it would feel so good? Okay, so I basically got rejected, but even initiating something on my own was freeing. Like the first time Jay and I kissed at the restaurant — I would have never started something like that with Mark. With him, I was always afraid to look stupid. Like if I made a move and put myself out there, he would pick me apart for trying to be sexy. There's just something about Jay that makes me feel like I can take control and not be judged for it. And for someone who is so used to being inside my head, that kind of dominance is empowering.

Glancing at the clock, I see it's already after midnight. Jay and I spent over two hours together, and I didn't even realize it until now. Time with him passes so fast, so easily. I could count on two hands how many days we've even known each other and yet, he's slowly becoming one of my favorite people — next to Chloe of course, who I promised I'd keep posted on any details. I shoot her a text telling her to call me tomorrow for updates.

Putting my pajamas back on, sans bra this time, I see in the mirror the spot where he marked my chest. Brushing my fingers over it, I'm hit with another wave of him. His gentle kiss on my neck, his callused hands running up my thighs, his possessive eyes on my bare skin. The heat between us was palpable, our bodies reacting to each other like one was flowing water and the other dying of thirst.

I crawl into bed hoping that considering the time, I can fall right to sleep but even now, just the memory of tonight keeps me awake. Lying in the same bed I brought him to, I can't help but imagine what it would have been like had he stayed.

His dropping to the floor between my legs is an image I don't want to forget. Would he have stayed there? Maybe slipped my shorts off next? Would he have trailed his lips up my inner thigh, until he reached my most sensitive spot? Would I have felt his breath beneath the fabric of my underwear as he swept it to the side? Would he have run his tongue up my middle until all that was left was for me to come undone?

Before I know it, my fingers find myself underneath my shirt. Picturing him where I miss him the most, they travel down to the same spot that he occupies in my mind. There, he's all mine. No interruptions, no audience, no sense of what's right or wrong. I get him all to myself, for whatever I want, as long as I want, and it's everything I've fantasized about since I first laid eyes on him.

In my mind, I get all of him.

And here alone, under my sheets, he gets all of me.

25

—

Jamison

Of course, I'm swamped at work today. I don't know what it is about Fridays but they're almost always nuts. The guys and I are cycling cars out of here one after another, barely taking even a ten-minute smoke break. To add to it, not only are we crazy busy, but we're also under a time constraint. Zeke must have forgotten when he strong-armed us all into going to Maddie's party, that most of us would have to put in a full day's work first. Not sure some of the guys will be in the mood for a party when we're done here.

I, on the other hand, can't fucking wait for Neon Nights. Add that to the list of things I never thought I'd say. But after last night, I'd go anywhere if it meant Claire would be there too. Speaking of things I never thought I'd say — *"I'm not going to do this."* What the hell was that? I'm so glad I decided to have a conscience then, at that exact moment.

After seeing her on that bed looking like a goddamn goddess, it took everything in me to get up and walk away from her. Figuratively and literally considering what I was sporting between my legs. It's an actual miracle I was able to move at all, but I had to. When I told her I wanted all of her, which even took me by surprise, I wasn't lying. It's the reason I texted her last night in the first place, to spend more time with her. So, I knew it was the right thing to do to leave before it got to that point but man, sometimes the hardest thing and the right thing are the same.

This girl drives me crazy. Mentally, physically, fucking emotionally, she makes me feel things I've never felt before. She makes me say things and do things I've never said or done before, but that's exactly why I wasn't willing to let her think I texted her just to get her into bed. Girls like Claire, want more than that. Hell, I want more than that, and if proving that means going home and taking care of things myself, then that's just what I'm going to do.

That's just what I did.

Now, I'm running around like a maniac and haven't had even a second to text her. It's not a good look, even I know that. No matter the reason, I left her shirtless on her bed last night and have yet to talk to her at all today. Definitely not ideal.

"Yo, buddy, you ready for tonight?" Sean calls from under the hood of the car next to the one I'm working on.

"Oh, I'm ready." It's a loaded answer but only to me.

"You bringing a present?"

Shit, I didn't even think of that. Do people still get grown adults gifts? I don't think I've ever gotten more than a few in all of my birthdays, so maybe I'm not the best judge.

"Should I? I haven't yet, but I guess I could stop somewhere on my way home."

"Ah, man, I've had my present ready to go for weeks now." He sounds way too eager about a gift he got for his boss's daughter. I roll my eyes but play along.

"What'd you get, Sean?"

He pops out from the hood with the biggest smile on his face. Talking with his hands he emphasizes every word.

"Pearl. Stud. Earrings."

I'm momentarily confused. Not because I don't know what pearl studs are but because I don't understand the significance of getting them for Maddie. Seeing my uncertainty, he explains.

"You know! Cause they're her birthstone."

Wow, that's actually crazy fucking nice.

Sean jokes around all the time about being into Maddie, but I always thought he was just doing it to get under Zeke's skin. Does he actually like her? He's younger than me so I guess it would only be weird because she's a Monroe. But, he has to — I didn't even get a gift and he bought possibly the most thoughtful one, not to mention, those things can't be cheap.

"That's cool, man. She'll love 'em."

"Damn straight! And wrapped in a purple bow. Her favorite color." He goes back to what he's working on, and I can't help but laugh. This guy is one of a kind.

<hr>

I make it back to my apartment with just enough time to shower and change. Thank God my outfit is already set. I stopped at the liquor store on the way home and picked up a bottle of very average tequila. Twenty-one-year-old girls are into that, right? At this point the answer is irrelevant. It's all I got, and I have to be at Claire's in twenty minutes if I want to be at Neon Nights when the party starts.

I rip the tags off of the jeans and t-shirt and throw them on. Despite how much I hate shopping, Ro was right. These look way better than my usual outfit. I remind myself to never, ever admit that to him and slide on the Vans that are also growing on me.

I take a look at myself in the mirror. The reflection I see *looks* different, but it *feels* different too. Call me crazy, but this girl gives me something to be excited about. Something to be hopeful for. Something I don't know that I've ever had before.

I grab my keys and the bottle of tequila and head out the door. I light a cigarette and the first rush of nicotine calms nerves I didn't even realize that I had. I mean it makes sense. I'm about to go out on my first official date with a girl who is way out of my league, whose father owns the car of my dreams, at a nightclub where if not now physically, at least mentally, I'll stick out like a sore thumb.

Instantly, I'm hit with a flashback.

I am barely nine years old and standing in the middle of the type of living room I've only ever seen in movies. They have ceilings that must be twelve feet high, a giant couch that runs the length of the house, and the biggest TV I have ever seen. Mel is in the kitchen next door talking to a couple with fancy names and fancy jewelry, and sitting on the giant couch are three kids — all well dressed, well groomed, and staring at me.

The oldest is a boy about my age, only we're complete opposites physically. Where my hair is ash blonde and overgrown, his is dark brown and clipped neatly by his ears. His clothes are clean and wrinkle-free. Mine are faded and there's a hole in the seam under one of my arms.

The other two are girls. One looks like she's maybe six or seven and the younger one is probably around three. She sits close to her big sister, hiding some sort of stuffed animal behind her back. Both girls are wearing matching dresses and have headbands that pull their hair neatly away from their faces.

"Why's he here?" the youngest girl whispers to the others.

"Looks like you need a bath," the boy says.

"Guys, Mom said to be nice." The oldest girl half-smiles at me but drops her face as soon as she sees my ripped-up sneakers.

Suddenly, I wish that my backpack, the only thing with me, was filled with helium, so I could float those twelve feet to the ceiling and away from these strangers.

The grown-ups come in, interrupting their comments and Mel puts her arm around me. "Jay, Mr. and Mrs. Carlisle are very excited to have you. You be a good boy, and I'll check in soon, okay?"

I hang my head. I met Mel yesterday when she told me she was from "The State," whatever that means, and that she was finding me a new place to live. This morning, she picked me up and took me for pancakes and french fries, and then brought me here. After everything you would think I'd be happy to move somewhere new — a fresh start. But not somewhere like this.

This isn't the type of place that I pictured when she told me she found me a "home." This isn't a home, it's a museum. I don't belong here. I don't fit into this perfect, little family in this perfect, giant house. What am I even supposed to say to these people? I can't even walk through their house without my ratty shoes dragging dirt onto their pure white carpet. I'm used to feeling alone, but not when I'm surrounded by other people.

The youngest girl pulls the stuffed animal she is holding out from behind her back, as Mel turns back to the Carlisles. The toy, that I can now see is some sort of lamb, is worn, parts of its fluffy white fur now matted over time, the color of butter. It's missing one eye, leaving a hole that has been roughly sewn shut and while one ear sticks straight out, the other now hangs down.

Holding the lamb against her body, the shabby stuffed animal stands out against the clear perfection of everything else — the faded yellow spots more obvious against the white of the little girl's dress. The mismatched ears, the only thing here not carefully set. And yet, even so, I am the most misplaced thing in the room. At least the toy is well-loved. It's wool raggedy from being hugged and held close and taken on real adventures. I, on the other hand, look tattered just because I am. Because, unlike the lamb, I have been left, rundown, and neglected. Because, unlike the lamb, I truly don't belong — the black sheep in this place I'm now supposed to call home.

I pull up to Claire's apartment and take one more deep breath before heading into her building. When I get to her door, I pause. There's music playing from the apartment, and I can hear her on the other side singing along to Pink's *Raise Your Glass*. I chuckle as I hear the lyrics. This girl is full of surprises. I'm tempted to sit here and listen to her belt out the rest of the song, but it's 8:45 pm and if we're late I might lose my job and my goddamn head to Zeke Monroe.

I knock loudly, all things considered, and hear her voice grow louder as she approaches the door. It isn't lost on me that she doesn't stop singing, and I love that she's that comfortable with me and herself. She times it perfectly, opening the door as she sings the last words of the hook about being so serious, with a dramatic frown on her face.

I close my eyes and smile at the irony of the words. She couldn't have planned this any better.

My eyes open and holy shit — she is fucking breathtaking. Her hair is pulled back on top of her head in a way that reminds me of the first day I saw her. She's wearing more makeup than usual, but she still looks like herself — dark lashes, pink cheeks — incredible.

As she stops the music on her phone, I scan the rest of her. My God. Her dress is black and lands halfway up her thighs. The neckline rises and falls across the front in a heart shape where her chest is and two tiny straps hold it up around her shoulders. Her shoes are simple black heels that wrap around her ankle, and it's only now that I realize she's standing at almost my height for once.

"You look..."

She does a slow twirl and it's only then that I see that her entire back is exposed, the cut of the dress dipping in a U shape to her hips. It's tasteful but so fucking sexy, and I suddenly wouldn't care if we we're late. Shit, I wouldn't care if we didn't go at all.

I blow out a heavy breath instead of finishing my thought.

"I'll take that as a compliment." She smiles and runs back inside grabbing a gold-wrapped bottle of champagne off the island. She hands it to me as she uses both hands to pull the door shut and lock it behind her. Grabbing the bottle again, she links her arm through mine as naturally as if we've done it a hundred times before.

And despite her ease, my stomach flips at just her skin on mine.

26

Claire

eon Nights is packed. We parked practically down the street just to avoid the chaos right out front, not that I mind it though. I am taking full advantage of the long walk hooked through Jay's arm.

We stand in a line just to get in and when it's our turn, we give the bouncer our name so he can check the list for Maddie's party.

"Dawson," I say.

He scans his list with the tip of his pen. I'm suddenly sweating for absolutely no reason because I know we're supposed to be here. It's like when I'm in airport security and all of a sudden I think, *Oh my God, did I pack a gun?*

"Claire Dawson, got it." He hands me a wristband in highlighter yellow and turns to Jay.

"Errington."

Once again his pen moves up and down his clipboard before it stops.

"Yep, Jamison Errington." He hands Jay the same bracelet. "Have a good night you two."

My head snaps to Jay whose brow is creased and ears are red. *Jamison.* Quick to end the moment, he places his hand on my lower back, a familiar touch from days before, and guides me through the door. I guess we will revisit that later.

Inside is even crazier than the front of the building. I must have forgotten what nightclubs are like because I am in total shock when I'm hit by a sea of sweaty people sloshing drinks in all directions. As if on instinct, Jay steps in front of me, a barrier between the chaos and me.

He slips his fingers through mine, and the rough spots on his palms play memories of those same hands sliding up my thighs. My body pulses beneath the skirt of my dress, and I squeeze his hand just a little tighter.

The house lights are dim with LEDs flashing colors as we push our way through the crowd toward the neon sign that says VIP. A dance remix of Rihanna's *Rude Boy* pounds through the speakers. We show the bouncer at the entrance our wristbands, and he steps aside to let us by. The VIP area is broken into sections, each one designated to a private party, with a large bar in the center. We both scan the room for any familiar face.

I see Maddie in a tiara and sash that says **Birthday Queen** and point her out to Jay. She looks great. She's wearing a pink sequin dress that's an inch too short and silver strappy heels that are an inch too high. The perfect outfit for a fresh twenty-one. Behind her I spot Zeke talking to a group of people I don't recognize but that all share familial similarities, maybe Maddie's aunts and uncles. At a cocktail table, Sean sits with Rick, and by the way Rick's hands are flailing, he seems to be telling a wild story, but instead of paying attention, Sean is staring at Maddie. Jay pulls me towards their table where we both set down our bottles.

Tearing his eyes from Maddie, Sean looks at us and his face lights up. "Hey! You're here!"

"We're here." Jay sounds about as thrilled as he looks with his furrowed brow and tightened lips. I knew this wouldn't be his scene as he said. It's not mine either, but it looks physically painful for him.

I squeeze his hand and whisper teasingly, "Fix your face. It's a party."

He looks down at our fingers interlaced, and dare I say he cracks a smile. I wink when our eyes meet again and now he's even showing teeth.

"Dude." Jay breaks our gaze to look at Sean who's talking again. "Do you see how good Maddie looks?"

Jay drops our hands to survey the room until he spots Maddie again, standing with her friends. "She looks nice."

"Nice?" Sean stands and places his hand on Jay's shoulder, leaning in to speak in chunks. "She is beautiful. Stunning. A work. Of. Art."

Jay claps him back on the shoulder and quickly replies, "She looks great, man. You want a drink, Claire?"

I can tell he's still a little overwhelmed by everything. Maybe a drink will relax us both. "I'll come with you," I say.

Jay checks with Sean and Rick to see if they need refills, which they do, and then we head to the bar.

The bartender is a tall blonde with boobs to her neck and shorts that might as well be underwear. She has on gold eyeliner and red lipstick and bops to the music as she mixes drinks. Jay leans across the bar to get her attention, which doesn't take much. When she spots him, she saunters over and lays her forearms on the counter. At this point, I'm not sure how she can even breathe with her tits practically in her throat, and yet, she somehow manages to also lick her lips and bat her lashes simultaneously. Multitasking at its finest.

"Ooh, I love me some tattoos. What can I get ya handsome?"

This can't be real. I feel like there's a stand-up comedy skit in the making here somewhere.

Jay looks at her overwhelmingly unimpressed. He orders a beer for Sean, club soda for Rick, a whiskey and water for himself, and then turns to me.

"I'll take a vodka soda, extra lime." Call me petty, but I lean just a little closer to Jay as I order.

Pam Anderson pushes off the bar with an eye roll and a crack of her gum, and Jay turns to me completely, elbow on the bar.

"What just happened there?"

"I believe you just got hit on."

He winces and swallows dramatically. "Yikes."

We both crack up laughing as the bartender returns with all four drinks.

Jay lays cash on the bar, grabbing mine and Rick's glasses, and handing them to me. He picks up Sean's beer and his drink and watches his admirer turn and sway away. He shivers dramatically in response.

Before I realize what I'm doing, I press a quick kiss to his lips the second he's turned around. I don't know if it's the slight, albeit ridiculous, jealousy or the fact that he seemed to have loosened up already, but I was drawn to show him even the slightest affection.
And there I go again, making the first move.

He stills with both hands full but his eyes seem to sparkle.

"Sorry," I laugh feeling a bit embarrassed. I realize after the fact that we've never kissed in public before and never so casually.

Jay steps forward, his expression more serious. "Don't you ever apologize for that."

He kisses *me* this time, only unlike my peck, he lingers. When he pulls back, his eyes are the perfect combination of completely satisfied and hungry for more. He nods in the direction of our section, and we both start walking toward our group.

Looking back over my shoulder I see the bartender pressing her goods together for the next guy. This one practically drools into her cleavage and lays a hundred on the counter.
I laugh as I follow Jay back to the party.

You do your thing girl. You do your thing.

27

Jamison

We've been here for almost an hour and I've gotten to talk to Claire for basically none of it. Besides the five minutes at the bar that ended way better than I could have planned, one of us has been talking to someone else the entire time. Luckily, we were each able to get our hands on another drink, in between introductions with this one and schmoozing with that one, to at least make the small talk tolerable for me.

Watching Claire interact with people from all walks of life is fascinating. For someone who has such a hard time socializing, it's wild to see it come so effortlessly to her. I was a witness to a few of her conversations and listening to her make small talk is like listening to Mozart play Symphony No. Whatever. It's fluid and easy and so damn detailed. This girl can ask a different question for every person she talks to and it's like each was handcrafted specifically for them. On top of it, she seems so genuinely interested in their answers. No other person in this world could sincerely ask Zeke what his favorite Chuck Berry song is *and* take an actual interest in his response.

After way too long without her, I finally catch a glimpse of Claire putting both of our bottles on the gift table, and for once, she's alone. I slip out of a useless conversation the guys from Monroe's are having about last year's WWE Wrestlemania and sneak up behind her. Before I make my presence known, I take just a second to once again admire her open back.

"I'm sorry, do I know you?" I tap her on the shoulder.

She turns, and before she responds, she looks me up and down. "Hmm, you know, I thought you might look like this guy I know, but he usually wears work boots." She drops her eyes to my shoes. "And, *he* goes by the name Jay." She smiles playfully. "Jamison was it?"

Hearing my full name spoken out loud feels so unfamiliar. Besides the few times that Zeke has said it just to annoy me, it's been years since I've answered to it.

The last time a woman spoke my full name was Mel. Despite aging out of the system, and no longer being a requirement, she and I have kept in touch. Well, more like she has kept in touch with me being that I don't reach out to anyone really. As sad as it is, she's been a constant in my life for longer than my own mother was, so I was glad when she didn't just disappear.

About three years ago Mel called me. This was strange in itself being that she mostly kept in contact through Christmas and birthday cards, but I always sent her my number and address if it ever changed.

"Hello?"

"Hey, Jay. It's me."

"What's up Mel? How've you been?"

"I'm good," she paused, *"Hey, listen..."* The way she took a deep breath, told me right away what was coming next.

"How?" I didn't need to hear her say it.

"Car accident. Completely sober if you can believe it."

I couldn't.

My whole life my mother struggled with either alcohol or men who struggled with alcohol. Decades of abuse both forced and self-inflicted. Thousands of nights hitting the bottle, dozens of nights being hit by men, and the way she goes is one of the most common ways to die.

You would think I'd have a more devastating response to finding out my mother was dead, but the truth was, I had prepared myself for this since I was old enough to know what death was. It's not something I'm proud of, but it was crucial to my survival. I realize it's not normal for a kid to grow up expecting to walk into their house and see their mom on the floor. It's not healthy for a child to put headphones in at night so they don't hear what could be their parent's last words, arguing with a man who's drunk and angry and twice her size. No, what it is, is a defense mechanism that readies you for the inevitable — or at least what you assume.

None of this is to say I didn't love my mom. I loved her unconditionally, the way a parent loves a child, despite her flaws and mistakes. Despite all of the times she let me down — but that's the problem. I wasn't the parent. I was the child. And sometimes I think she forgot that the roles weren't reversed.

All of this to say, now is not the time to drop this piece of me on Claire. But because I can't just leave it completely, I offer something different.

"Yes. Jamison is my full name. I obviously had to fill out all of my paperwork for Zeke when he hired me, and he likes to throw it around every once in a while just to piss me off." I take another step closer to her. "But Jay is just fine."

Claire tilts her head to one side and puts her finger to her lips. "I don't know," she says, moving in one more step. "I kind of like Jamison."

"Yeah…" I finish closing the gap between us. Thanks to her heels, we now stand face to face and chest to chest. "I really don't."

"Well," she says looking to my lips, "What are you going to do about that…Jamison?"

With that, I press my mouth to hers. This kiss, unlike those at the bar, is deeper, harder, and heated. Fueled by my attraction to her and the sting of my most recent memory. I normally wouldn't do something like this in public but A. It's dark as Hell in here and B. At this point, I don't really give a shit.

I wrap one hand around her hip and the other around the back of her head, claiming all of her as mine. She fists my shirt with both hands, a soft moan escaping from her throat. All of the blood that's been pumping through my chest rushes south. I lean into her to increase the pressure between us, but she bumps into the table of presents instead.

We both smile beneath our kiss and she breaks away first, hiding her face in the crook of my neck. "So, not Jamison. Got it."

I practically snort at the shift in climate, and she giggles into me before pulling back, wiping her bottom lip with her thumb.

I clear my throat dramatically and pull at my jeans. Have I mentioned I'm so glad it's fucking dark in here? The opener of *Wild Ones* starts playing and Sia's voice fills the club. Claire's eyes tell me before her words do — she loves this goddamn song.

"No."

Claire nods her head.

"No," I persist.

She grabs my hand. "Yes!" and drags me through the VIP.

When we leave the private area it's like a whole other world. The DJ to the left is lifted on a mini stage spotlighted in changing colors. The bar to the right runs the length of the building, wrapping even around the corner to the other side. The dance floor in the middle is just a sea of people, bobbing and swaying to the beat of the music.

I stop abruptly, causing Claire, who is leading, to be pulled back to me. She can't possibly want to go into the middle of this mob scene. I'm bumped twice by people trying to push their way through and even that is enough contact for me to know there is no way in Hell I'm stepping foot into *that*.

She must see the overwhelm on my face because just as Flo Rida's voice bellows through the speakers, Claire starts to dance. Right here, at the edge of the crowd, she throws her hands in the air and starts jumping to the beat. She's pumping her fists and spinning around, and the smile on her face makes this mayhem worthwhile. I shove both hands in my pockets and let her do her thing.

Never in my life did I think I'd ever be here — in a packed club, with someone who despite all she seems to have going on, can just put it aside and be this carefree. I could get lost in watching her twirl around, but suddenly Sia is back with the chorus, and she slows down her movements and glides over to me. Mouthing the words, she throws her arms around my neck, and I'm lost in this feeling of just being a part of something right now. It's so damn corny, but Claire makes me feel a sense of belonging that's entirely new to me.

As the music picks back up, my arms, which I have around her lower back, start to bounce with her dancing again. Then suddenly my shoulder jolts forward, but not because I'm feeling the beat. I look at Claire who is covering her mouth hiding her laughter at whatever is behind me. Turning, I see a very drunk Sean leaning on a very irritated Rick. He smacks my shoulder one more time and puts a source to the movement.

Claire and I both drop our arms as Sean's lips begin moving, but no sound can be heard over the bass of the speaker. I point to the private area, and we all cross back into the VIP section. The music softens just slightly this far removed from the main floor and Sean speaks again.

"She's dancing, Jay." His words come out slurred.

Claire and I look at each other confused. Rick holds up a finger telling us to wait.

"She's dancing with some big tall guy like you." He pokes my chest, then points to his own. "My girl."

Understanding washes over me and I turn to Claire, mouthing *"Maddie."* Her eyebrows shoot up and then settle in a crease as if she's now both confused and surprised. I nod in agreement knowing exactly how she's feeling.

I lean into her and whisper, "He's stupid drunk. Do you mind if I walk him outside and figure this shit out?" She shakes her head no and grabs my hand. When I said that, I didn't mean for her to come with me, but there she goes making me feel like I'm not alone again.

Rick throws Sean's arm around my other side, and the three of us make our way to the VIP's back exit to the outside of the club. I didn't realize I needed fresh air until it hit me, but once we opened the doors, it was like my lungs filled fully for the first time all night.

I sit Sean on the curb, and Claire sits next to him. I stand in front of them both, reaching for my cigarettes. I notice Claire's eyes on my movement as I glide one back, forth, back across my lips, and settle it off to the side, right as Sean whines again.

"What am I going to do, guys? I love her!"

Claire sticks out her bottom lip and rubs Sean's back. This girl is a fucking angel.

And he is a pathetic mess.

"Have you ever even talked to her? I mean like, does she know you exist?" I'm not trying to be a dick, I'm just trying to see what we're dealing with here.

Sean looks at me like I have six heads and then asks Claire, "Is he talking cursive to you too, or just me?"

Claire bursts out laughing and I pause mid-drag.

"Alright, you're done here." I put out a perfectly good cigarette for this clown and hoist him up under his arms like a goddamn baby.

"I can throw him in a cab."

Claire, who's now standing too, shakes her head. "No way, he'll never make it. Where does he live?"

"Right by me."

Her face drops just slightly enough that I notice. "Why don't you take me first and then drop him off on your way home."

"No," I say but she's already nodding her head. It's like the dancing thing all over again only this time it's way less cute.

"Claire."

"Jamison." We both smirk at the name.

"I'm not spending the rest of my night with this asshole instead of you." Sean looks at me like now all of a sudden he knows what I'm saying. "No offense, buddy." He leans his head against my arm.

Claire pouts again and pats him on the head like the sad little puppy that he is. "It's fine Jay, seriously."

It is so not fine, but what else am I supposed to do with him? If I leave him here, he'll get kicked out, or worse, and I'm not having that on my conscience too.

I shrug Sean's head off of my shoulder with a huff like a kid who didn't get his way. Holding his face in my hands I look him in the eye. "Stay here," I insist.

Claire steps next to him, taking over the babysitting while I pull the truck around. Looking back, I see Sean's head now resting on her arm in the same way it was on mine.

This guy so fucking owes me.

28

Claire

As much as it killed me to end our night short again, Sean is in a rough spot. When we got in Jay's truck he told us about how he's been in love with Maddie for a year now. Ever since she stopped by the garage to drop Zeke's phone off once when he forgot it and told him he looked like a ginger Zach Galifianakis. I'm personally not sure if she meant that as a compliment, but if that's how Sean took it, who am I to burst his bubble?

Either way, I would hate to be him tomorrow morning. He's currently sitting in the back with his head against the window singing. He just keeps repeating the part in the Richard Marx song about how he'll wait for his lover even after his heart breaks, horrendously offkey.

I'm riding shotgun, with my window down, trying not to either laugh or sing along, and Jay is driving with both hands white-knuckling the wheel.

It's kind of adorable watching him be so mad at Sean, while also taking care of him. I know he's upset that our night took a turn but seeing him still be there for his friend, honestly just makes me want him more. I put my hand on his leg, and his eyes dart from the road to my hand, then back to the road.

"I hate this," he says, grinding his teeth.

"You're a good friend."

"I don't *want* to be a good friend. I *want* to be with you."

I squeeze his thigh, and he lets out a growl. Not like a sexy groan, an actual growl. This guy is so grumpy about this and I'm loving every second of it. We pull up to my apartment just as Sean is finishing his performance.

Jay gets out of the truck and comes around to my door. Opening it, he lets me out and then sticks his head in, talking to Sean. "Do not puke. I'll be right back." He slams the door shut.

I look at him and my mind funnels through all of the things I'd rather him do than get in his truck and leave. I saw such a different side of him tonight. The bones were still there — his straightforward answers, hidden smiles, and strong, stoic nature. But new layers also came to light. We flirted together, kissed in public, and danced along with everyone. Okay, I danced along with everyone, but he stood there, my one-man audience, like I was the best show in town. I had such a good time with him, and at least in my mind, it wasn't going to end on my doorstep.

"I can walk you in, but I'm kind of afraid he's going to make a run for it." Jay looks back at Sean who is blowing breaths on the window and writing Maddie's name in the fog. He drops his head, turning back to me. "I'm really sorry about this."

"Don't be sorry. It happens."

"Yeah, but things *keep* happening." He steps forward and takes both of my hands in his. "And not the things I want to be happening."

I can feel my face grow warm. I step forward and kiss him as my response. He parts his lips, and I sweep my tongue inside to meet his. He kisses me again and then pulls back.

"Okay, if I don't stop now," he looks over his shoulder to Sean. "He'll end up sleeping in my truck."

"Well, you could always leave snacks. Maybe crack a window?"

He laughs and then grows serious. "I'll see you tomorrow." It's not a question.

"Okay."

"Dinner. Like an actual date."

"Ooh we go could go to—"

"Not at Enzo's."

I close my mouth mid-sentence, turning in my lips.

"I'll text you a plan. Seven?"

"I'll be here."

"You better be."

He leans in, but last minute, kisses only my cheek leaving my lips completely abandoned.

"I had a great night, Claire. Until well..." He looks back at Sean who is asleep, drool dripping down the window.

"Me too." I bite my lower lip but my stomach swirls with the anticipation of us going out again.

He starts for his truck but stops at the driver's side door, scanning me one more time from head to toe.

"Perfect."

I tilt my head curiously.

"Earlier — I never finished my thought. You look fucking perfect."

He misses the fire he starts inside of me because he starts the engine and drives away.

An arsonist escaping the scene of the crime.

"Sorry, I'm late." Chloe slumps in the seat across from me and throws her bag on the table, just barely missing the mocha cold brew that's waiting for her.

"Long night?" I wink at her taking a mouthful of my drink and noticing the slight smear of mascara she has under both eyes.

"Yeah...alone." She takes three long sips of her coffee. "I seriously have to either stop going on shitty dates or stop getting drunk by myself afterward."

"Uh oh, Motorcycle Guy was no good?"

She looks at me disgusted. "*Motorcycle* Guy was more like *Moped* Guy. And I'm not talking like *cruising around Europe* moped. I'm talking like a bicycle with a freaking motor on the back."

I nearly spit out my drink as she continues.

"He showed up wearing white jeans that looked painted on and drew way too much attention to his very below-average bulge. Then, he casually dropped that he lives with his sister in a one-bedroom apartment and he *still* tried to kiss me at the end of the night."

"Yikes," I say.

"Open-mouthed, Claire. He tried to kiss me with an open mouth." She shudders at the thought.

I am dying, but I pull it together and ask seriously, "So, no second date then?"

"Very funny. I dodged the kiss and walked right back into the bar." She scrolls through her phone and then turns it to me. "I got this about an hour later."

KYLE: Was it the pants...?

This is too good.

Chloe pulls her phone back and throws it in her bag. "Please tell me your night went better than mine."

I'm not convinced that Chloe wants anything serious, but these guys she meets online are always of a rare breed. It almost feels like rubbing it in to say that my super hot date looked absolutely smoking in jeans that looked made for him and his very impressive bulge.

So, instead, I just say, "It was fun!"

"Ugh, I hate you for having a regular, boring boyfriend."

Probably way too quickly I clarify. "He's not my boyfriend." *And he's definitely not boring from what I've seen so far.*

"Oh please." She drinks more of her coffee which at this point is almost gone. "You've seen each other like every day since you've met and he's totally into you."

I smile at the thought. Technically only about half of the times we've seen each other were both intentional and mutual, but I mean, I'm not a prude, I know Jay is interested. I guess hearing it from my best friend just hits differently.

"Plus you're like putty in his hands so..."

I roll my eyes and kick her leg under the table. She's not entirely wrong there either. In this last week and a half, Jay and I have grown closer than I would have ever imagined when I saw him that first day. Who would have thought the sexy guy with muscles and tattoos would end up also being sweet and a really good listener? Now I know what people mean when they talk about falling fast. I think when it comes to Jay, he's a cliff and I sort of nosedived right off.

"So what's going on with the car?"

The question of the year. I was on the phone with Mom on my way here. She was complaining about the car taking up so much space in the garage that she was going to take a sparkler out of the Fourth of July box she was looking for and shove it somewhere I'm pretty sure a car doesn't have.

"Beats me. Last I heard he had turned down another offer because as the man pulled up, a black cat walked in front of his van. Dad called it bad luck and told the poor guy to leave. If you ask me, I think he has cold feet on selling it altogether."

"Oh, Tommy boy." Chloe has this thing with names and refuses to call my dad Tom like a normal person. It borderline makes me uncomfortable.

"Can you please not call him that?"

"Listen, Big Tom just needs to sell the thing to the highest bidder. Sentiment won't matter once the money hits the account."

"Damn Chlo, that's kinda cold."

She rubs her forehead. "I know, I'm sorry. I tend to get a little ganglordy when I'm hungover."

Chloe might be the most dramatic person I've ever met, but that's exactly why I love her.

"Why don't you go sleep it off, Gambino."

She flips me a middle finger and a smile and grabs her bag off the table.

"Keep me posted on the boy and the car, okay?"

"Deal." I blow her a kiss as she walks out the door.

I'm finishing the last few sips of my butterscotch latte when my phone buzzes with a text from a number I don't know. I swipe the message open.

UNKNOWN: Hey Claire, it's Maddie! I made Dad give me your number. Here are some pics the photographer at my party got of you and Jay. So cute. Thanks for coming! Xoxo

Attached to the message are two pictures of Jay and I.

The first is of the two of us by the gift table. The viewpoint is of our sides as we're standing, talking to each other. This was right before *the* kiss when I called him Jamison for the first time. I still can't believe I didn't even consider that Jay may not be his full name.

I'm grinning in Busy's as I look at the picture. Man, we look great together. Our matching black with his shirt and my dress, and the contrast of his inked skin versus my blank canvas. We're both wearing casual smiles, but even in the subtly we look genuinely happy.

The second picture is entirely different. It looks like this one was taken from the entrance to the VIP section. The two of us are just barely out the doors on the edge of the main dance area. My eyes go to Jay's powerful figure, and all I see is his tall, broad, back. Both hands are predictably in his pockets and I can't say I'm complaining about the view. Then, I see myself.

I'm in front of Jay, just slightly off to the side so that you can see me in the frame. My hands are in the air, my eyes closed, mouth open, and I know from the memory that I'm belting the words to the song in the background. This girl looks...serene. She doesn't look weighed down by life changes or job decisions. And she doesn't look like she's overthinking the entire situation. She looks light and relaxed. She looks carefree.

Before our first kiss, Jay told me I wouldn't want someone like him. For some reason, he sees himself as damaged. Like whatever has happened to him in the past has left him broken. But that's not what I see.

I see a guy allowing the girl in this picture to finally feel like herself. A version of her that's been hidden by stress and worry — by anxiety and overthinking. A version that doesn't look burdened at all by his baggage.

No, I see a guy who despite his "brokenness," makes the girl in this photo feel more whole than she ever has before.

29

Jamison

I made a reservation for 7:30 pm at the nicest place in town, which by definition is still not anything spectacular. Proseccos is one of the only restaurants in Maple Grove that doesn't have a takeout menu with tearable coupons posted inside. That's not to say it's winning any Michelin Stars anytime soon either, but it's the most lavish place I could think of that would have prime-time reservations still available the day of. Regardless, any place where the waiter isn't also the bartender isn't really my cup of tea. To be honest, I'm not sure it's Claire's either, but I'm new to this and thought I'd air on the side of caution.

Naturally, I had absolutely nothing that would qualify as fucking "fancy enough" to wear to this place, so I asked Mikey to help me out. Normally I would call Ronan for this type of thing, but being that he's almost half a foot shorter than me, I thought his taller brother might be a better fit.

According to Mikey, I can wear "nice jeans," as long as I wear a blazer. A goddamn blazer. I knew there was a reason I never did this shit. Luckily Mikey, much like his brother, is a little bit of a clothes snob and has a black one he's letting me borrow that he says should fit fine. I'll pair it with the only button-up I own, which thank God just happens to be white and matches everything, and my black Vans and call it a day. I don't care what anyone says, I'm not wearing dress shoes to eat goddamn spaghetti.

I'm actually off for once on a Saturday, but I came to Monroe's still for just a couple of hours. When I dropped Sean off last night at his apartment, I already knew that he wouldn't make it in on time today. It may have had something to do with having to practically carry him to the door or him thanking the Jay *next* to me for doing it, but either way, I left a text on his phone saying I'd cover him until lunch. Have I mentioned this dickhead owes me big time?

It's relatively slow today. Zeke purposely got rid of half our appointment slots, knowing that even he would be out late the night before. Rick, the only other guy in right now, is working on the one car in the garage. Zeke, who was "cutting loose" while everything went down, doesn't even know that we left early, and I plan to keep it that way. Sean can put **Not telling our boss he spiraled because Zeke's only daughter isn't in love with him** on my tab for what he owes me.

For the last half hour, I have been listening to Zeke bullshit about the party and every interaction that he had, when I finally ask the question I've been thinking about for days — if only to shut him up about everything else.

"So, have you heard anything about the Maverick?"

He looks at me sideways. "You haven't? I thought now that you and Claire were an item that you'd be all over that information." I guess he's right, I could ask her. But I don't want her to think I'm hanging out with her for information on the car.

"Okay, first of all, the term "item" is fucking weird. Second of all...Claire and I aren't...that." *At least not officially. Not yet.*

"You two looked pretty cozy last night." He does this shoulder-shrug thing that I can never unsee. And yeah, maybe I could have brought it up last night, but it's not really a nightclub conversation. What was I supposed to do? Scream over the bass of Cat Daddy, "Hey! Anyone buy the car your dead grandfather left your dad who thinks it's a huge pain in the ass?"

"Zeke, the car?"

"Okay, okay. No, I haven't heard much. Apparently, Claire's dad has been hemming and hawing with all of the offers he's gotten so far."

"You think he's deciding to keep it?"

"Nah, I just think it's harder for him to let it go than he realizes."

I nod my head in understanding. I'm glad to hear that the car is finally getting some of the respect that it deserves. When I first heard the owner, who I now know is Claire's dad, wanted to get rid of it, I couldn't believe how easily he would just pass it to the best offer. But the fact that he's being so critical about who he'll sell it to, makes me feel better about watching it slip away.

Claire hasn't talked about her family much. I know she's an only child, but we haven't gotten to her parents yet. To be honest, I just kind of assumed her dad was just a money guy looking for the biggest payout. From what Zeke said about not wanting to be lowballed and hearing Claire say there was interest but still no sale, I just assumed. Now, I'm wondering, like Zeke, if there's maybe more to it.

Zeke tosses a hand towel at me, grabbing my attention back. "Thinking about throwing your hat in the ring?"

I snort at just the thought. "Yeah, right. I can't even store that thing let alone afford it. Where would I park it? Out back, next to the dumpster?"

Zeke laughs, but even he knows it's true. In this small of a shop, we all get to know each other's stories. At least bits and pieces of them.

When I aged out at eighteen, I really had nowhere to go. After years of being told where I was going to stay, I finally had the freedom to decide where to live and had no idea where to do it. The only logical thing to me was to go to the place where the only real family I ever had was, and that was here in Maple Grove with the Carusos. Mr. and Mrs. Caruso let me stay in their guest room for the better part of a year before the boys decided to open their shop. With the help of their dad, who had long since left the restaurant business, but was still a *"Pizzaiolo at heart"* as he would say, they got this place up and running before Ronan could legally drink.

It was a shock to me when the boys offered me this place to stay. They knew how much it was killing me to stay with their family for free. Mrs. Caruso refused to accept money for rent, so instead, I'd keep the fridge stocked with the foods I knew they ate the most and tried to get odd jobs done around the house. That combined with how close it was to

Monroe's where I had just started to work, they thought it'd be the perfect solution, and it was.

All that to say, it was supposed to be temporary. But with being so busy with work and not having much of a reason to leave, I have taken advantage of the low rent and easy access to my best friends, despite sometimes feeling like a charity case who has overstayed his welcome.

Walking over to me, Zeke puts a reassuring hand on my shoulder. As much as he and I give each other shit, we've known each other for years. He knows my situation and how I feel about it.

Squeezing my shoulder, all he says before heading to the office is, "No one season lasts forever, Jay."

I'm standing out back behind my apartment with a cigarette and a cup of coffee before I have to start getting ready for tonight. The sky is dull and it finally isn't a million degrees out. Apparently, they're calling for a "summer storm" tonight, which I've never understood. We don't call it a fall or winter storm, so how come when the same thing happens in the warmest months, we call it something special? Regardless, we could use the relief. I just wish that the first rainfall we've had in two weeks wasn't going to fall on the same night as my first real date with Claire. I'm far from a superstitious guy, but this just feels like some kind of bad omen from a universe that otherwise has kind of been on my side for once.

Luck aside, this kind of weather always takes me back to that day. Gray skies, muggy air, the sun trying its best to show its face but failing. One of the worst days of my life happened before a summer storm. So much for the calm before.

My phone ringing in my pocket brings me back to the now. Putting out my cigarette, I reach for it, to see Mikey's name lit up on the screen.

"Yo."

"Amico! I'm here. Just hung the jacket on your door. I got deliveries real quick though, so I can't hang."

"Cool, cool, you comin' back?"

"I'll be in and out. If I don't see you before, good luck tonight."

"Yeah man, thanks. And thanks for the jacket."

"You got it, brother."

I hang up the phone and check the time.

Before sliding it back into my pocket, I shoot Claire a text to make sure she's still good for seven. I get a reply almost immediately.

CLAIRE: Still good :)

I make the cheesiest smile and for once I'm so glad that my backyard is an empty parking lot.

30

Claire

"Jesus Christ, Claire, it is pouring right now." Chloe, who may be more excited about my date than I am, sits on speakerphone while I finish putting on my makeup.

"And on the one day I actually straightened my hair."

"Nooo," she says dramatically, rifling through something on the other end of the phone.

"Let's just hope it stops long enough for me to enter and exit the car without looking like a drowned rat." I comb my fingers through my freshly ironed hair as if willing it to stay this way.

"May the odds be ever in your favor," she says in her best Effie Trinket.

"You get me," I say, swiping one last coat of mascara to my already dark lashes.

It's an anxious tick of mine. Whenever I'm going somewhere important or special, I always apply way too many coats of mascara, as if the long, thick lashes will catch all of my nervous energy like flies to a web.

"What time is he coming over?" Chloe mumbles, clearly eating something very unladylike. I look at the time - 6:40 pm.

"Twenty minutes."

"Are you dressed yet?"

"About to be." I put down the mascara and walk away before my eyelids are too heavy to lift.

"Ooh. Switch me. To Skype. So I can see. The whole look," she says while crunching in between words.

"Yeah, I'm not going to do that. And what the hell are you eating?"

"Celery with peanut butter," she says earnestly.

I laugh. "What are you, five?"

"I have to go grocery shopping!" she snaps. "Besides, you tell me ants on a log aren't *still* delicious."

I roll my eyes and shake my head. "You're one of a kind Chlo."

"I luh ya too," she responds, mumbling again. "Caw me tomorrah!"

"You got it." She hangs up, but not before crunching even louder one last time in my ear, definitely on purpose.

I go to my closet and pull out my dress. All Jay told me was that we were going to dinner. Technically that could be at Taco Bell for all I know, but I decided to get at least one more wear out of this dress anyway. If it is Taco Bell then, yo quiero...still wear this dress.

I first bought it for the end-of-the-year banquet at Jefferson. Silly me thought I could use it as my annual celebratory dress.
Turns out I can, just only one time.

It's a deep red satin, and sleeveless, falling just above my knee. It's classy, especially when paired with a cardigan and flats, which is what I did for work, but on its own, or matched with metallic gold heels and dangly earrings, it can be elevated to look way more sexy — which is how I'm wearing it now.

Looking at myself in the mirror, I don't clean up half bad. Sure, I could probably afford to trim off some dead ends, and the dress hugs my runner's thighs a little too tightly, but overall, I'd say, not too shabby.

I am transferring my cell phone, ID, and credit card, to my gold-beaded clutch, when I hear a knock at the door. Glancing at the time again, I see it's 7:00 pm on the dot.

"Come in!" I call as I shove lip gloss and a pack of gum into my purse just in case.

I'm walking through my bedroom door, struggling with the snap of the clutch when I hear the door click open. Looking up from this purse, which is totally fighting back, I see Jay, in an open blazer, absolutely drenched. Which of those two things surprises me more? I'm not sure.

I drop my purse on the loveseat and pull my hand to my mouth. "Oh my God," I say, the words muffled by my palm.

"It's raining." He says bluntly.

"I see that." I walk towards where he stands in my doorway, dripping from head to toe. Detouring to the hall closet, I pull out a towel. I hand it to him as he steps aside so I can close the door behind him, and he immediately brings it to his hair, droplets spraying every which way from the short bristles of his cut. As he drags the towel down his face, he pauses, still covering the lower half. He stares at me, drinking me in. The towel slowly falls as he starts to speak.

"Claire, you look incredible."

I feel myself grow warm from both his stare and the compliment.

"Incredibly...dry?" I try lightening the mood because I'm nervous already, and the way that he so easily shuts down all of my insecurities, only makes it worse.

"No," he says instantly. "I had it right the first time." He looks down at his completely soaked body. "But also, yes."

I smile and take the opportunity to look him up and down myself. He's in jeans and Vans, which I've seen before, but damn. Jay in a white shirt and blazer is a whole different look. His button-up is wet down the middle where his blazer fell open in the storm and the fabric clings to his muscles underneath in the best possible way. He has his jacket sleeves pushed up so his forearms show, his tattoos glistening on his damp skin, and the way it hugs his biceps is intoxicating.

He looks so good. Uncomfortable honestly, but so freaking sexy.

He catches me checking him out and the corner of his lips turn up. I snap out of my Jay-induced haze just long enough to reach for his jacket.

"Here, let me help you take this off." I wince at how that sounds. "I mean let's get you out of these clothes." *Much better.* "Just...here."

I pull each flap over his shoulder as he shrugs out of the sleeves. Laying the jacket carefully over the island to dry, I turn back to the mouth-watering picture that is Jay in a wet, white, button-down shirt. If

I thought the sliver of exposed fabric was sexy before, getting the full picture is in another league.

We both look at each other with a mixture of attraction and hesitance, the mood in the room suddenly heavy. I walk over to him, unable to fight the pull I feel and place my hands on his damp chest. Moving my fingers to his first button, I pause.

"Do you want to let this dry a little before we leave?" My voice comes out huskier than intended.

He looks down at me, not quite his height in these heels, his hazel eyes wide from the angle.

"Okay," is all he says.

I undo the button, my hands trembling just enough that I can feel it but there's no visible movement. His shirt falls open slightly more after it comes undone, the lines of his chest muscles greeting me on either side.

I move my hands to the second button, and Jay lets out a heavy breath. Peering up at him, I see he's not looking at his shirt at all, but staring directly at me. I fumble with the button, eventually undoing it, my chest practically touching his now bare skin with every heaving breath.

Unconsciously, I move closer to him, my thighs skimming his, so I can feel his wet jeans through the fabric of my dress. I slide my hands down over the peaks of his muscles. He sucks in a sharp breath as goosebumps cover his flesh, and just seeing his reaction to my touch, makes the spot between my thighs come alive.

Trailing my palms down to where his shirt still sits closed, I move to the final button. I feel him harden between us as I pinch my fingers around the clear, white, plastic at the same time that Jay rips it open. He drops his shirt and grabs my face in one swift motion, pulling my lips to his. As if on cue, I move my hands to his hair and pull on the back of his head to deepen our embrace. It's wet and messy, now matching our clothes, and all I can seem to think is *more*. More touching, more kissing, more clothes on the ground.

With our mouths still interlocked, I reach for his collar, pulling his shirt off of his shoulders in the same way I did with his jacket, only this time, I throw it right to the floor. With his upper half fully exposed, I run my hands down his arms, feeling the flex and release of his muscles as he moves his hands, first to my waist and then lower behind me. We're both eagerly exploring, frantic to pull our bodies even closer together.

At this point, I think it's safe to say that dinner's off. I for one, am no longer hungry for anything but more of him. I pull back long enough to say one word.

"Bedroom."

He nods without breaking our next kiss, his tongue impatiently finding mine once again. Unexpectedly, he spins me around, my back pressed against him. I arch, increasing the pressure, and he groans in my ear before brushing his teeth down my neck. My hand finds the back of his head again, pushing him harder against my skin, even further deepening his touch. The sound that escapes me would be embarrassing at any other time, but the way he twitches underneath me, tells me I have nothing to worry about.

He brings one hand to my jaw, turning my face towards him again. Sucking on my lower lip, his hand finds my chest. I whimper, and the moan he makes in response is everything. I decide right then that I want to spend the rest of my night trying to pull that sound out of him over and over again.

I finger the strap of my dress and slowly pull it down. He pauses his kiss, watching me release my arm from the fabric, then mirroring my movement on the other side until my chest is all that holds it in place. Stepping forward, creating space between us for the first time, I shimmy my dress down, revealing the back of my black strapless bra. Almost instantly, Jay's soft lips are on my shoulder.

"Jesus, Claire." He plants gentle kisses around the curve.

Turning back to look at him, I continue pulling the material further down, revealing a band of black lace around my hips. Jay's hands find mine and guide them over the last hurdle, gravity pulling the dress to a pile on the floor.

Now it's him who creates distance. Stepping back, Jay drags a hand down his face taking in my curves. I extend an arm back and he slips his hand in mine.

Pulling him to my room, I'm reminded of the first time I brought him to bed. A wave of anxiety rolls through me thinking of the last time I was vulnerable here with him. I spin around, suddenly feeling even more exposed than I already am. Avoiding his gaze, I bring one arm across my chest, rubbing the area just below my shoulder. Sensing my energy shift, Jay glides close.

"Hey." He tilts my chin and studies my face. "I'm not going fucking anywhere."

The mere idea that he can calm my brain without me having to even explain myself is enough to undo me right then and there. I reach for the top of his jeans, pulling the belt loops like I did before. There's that feeling of empowerment again.

Still holding the loops, I kiss the crook of his neck. Dragging my tongue from the base to his ear, I nibble gently, then whisper, "Off."

He throws his head back in response.

"Fuck, Claire." It comes out so quietly I almost miss it.

He brings his fingers to his button, then unzips them to expose the waistband underneath. As they fall to the floor, the length of him springs to life, straining against his briefs, two muscular thighs bulging as he kicks them to the side.

My God, this man is beautiful. He stands in front of me, a pillar of strength, and I want to drop to my knees and worship him. But before I can make my move, he makes his first.

"Lay down, Claire."

31

Jamison

I watch as Claire sits back on her bed in only her bra, thong, and those sexy gold heels. The last time we were here, I willed myself to leave. This time, no force on this planet could rip me from these goddamn walls.

Watching her undress was fucking intoxicating. The confidence mixed with that body drove me crazy and when she took control and whispered in my ear to take off my jeans, I thought a strong wind might finish me off right there.

But not yet. Not before I show her how truly perfect she is.

I walk to her slowly, savoring the view. She leans back on her forearms putting her chest on full display. I kneel between her legs and run my palms up her thighs in the same motion as I did only nights before. But this time, I'm not stopping there.

Gliding my hands back down her flawless figure, I move to one ankle, slowly working the strap of her heel until I can easily slide it off. I kiss the soft arch of her foot, then repeat the process on the other side. Claire points and flexes each foot, her body responding to my touch. I toss both shoes aside and work my mouth back upwards.

Claire mentioned that she runs, but holy shit these legs. They're smooth and strong, and combined with the early summer tan already tinting her skin, I don't think I could have molded them more perfectly myself. When I reach the top of her thighs, I pause at her middle. I sigh a warm breath and Claire shifts her hips.

"Jay," She looks down at me. "You don't have to."

I can practically see her wheels spinning. I don't know who she was with before, but if anyone ever made her feel like this was a chore, they're the biggest dumbass I've ever met.

"I know I don't have to." I pull down the lace on both sides, the force causing her to sink deeper to me. I inhale loudly at just the sight of her. I shouldn't be surprised that she's perfect here too. "But trust me, baby, I'm doing this for me too."

I run one finger down her slit and she squirms in response. She is so fucking wet. My tongue finds her next, and I don't just taste her, I devour her. Licking and sucking, I cater to her like I haven't eaten in days. When I feel her legs tighten around me, I slip two fingers in, filling her and pushing her to the edge.

"Oh my God," she cries out. "Oh my..." Her legs start to quiver, and as I suck one last time on her most sensitive spot, she free-falls.

She comes down from her high, her breath ragged. I stand, looking down at her now limp body. She sits up, still panting.

"Okay, that was," She pauses searching for the word. "Transcendent."

I drop my head and laugh. "You're such an English teacher."

"Come here," she says more seriously.

She frees me from the material, her hand curling around my length. I haven't been touched like this in so long and never by someone I cared for like her. I let out a low groan and she shifts forward, parting her lips.

"Wait," I say in a hushed tone. Her eyes dart to mine, confused. "It's been a long time, Claire. Like a really fucking long time." I lean forward causing her to lay back down in response. "And if you touch me like that, I'm going to fall apart before I even get to be inside you." I give her one hard, wet, kiss. "And I *need* to be inside you."

Claire gasps, reaching for me. I stumble all but on top of her, my briefs half up, half down, and we both let out a laugh. Laying on my side, next to her all but naked body, I pull her to me and she turns in naturally. I land on the bare skin between her thighs practically reaching for my prize. Growing almost instantly serious, we collide again, only stopping when Claire quietly utters the single most delicious sound.

"Please."

Despite being exactly what I want, I hesitate, pulling back from our embrace. It hits me that if we do this, there's no undoing it. I will want her with everything I have, and she will be somehow attached to everything I don't. I close my eyes trying to muster the courage to question this. To make sure that she knows she is giving a piece of herself to an absolute mess.

"I want this, Jay." She speaks before I have the chance. "Please."

There's that word again. She leans in, but I keep the distance.

Ripping off the bandaid, I respond. "Claire, I'm so fucking broken." At this point, she has enough of the pieces to understand what I'm saying, even if she's still missing a few.

She pulls her head back furrowing her brow. "You're not broken, Jay." I exhale heavily, closing my eyes.

"Trust me, I am."

She drops her forehead to mine, our noses just barely touching. I feel her breath on my lips, warm and sweet, just like her.

"Then be broken." She lifts her head and my heart sinks. I wince, at the lack of contact, my chest heavy with regret.

I hear her speak but my inner thoughts half-drown out the faint sound of her voice. My eyes shoot open.

"What?"

"With me," she repeats. "I said, then be broken. With me."

I press my mouth to hers urgently, the words I have for her spoken in pressure. I hold that kiss, getting myself together. Giving myself time to swallow the lump in my throat, that she put there with two simple words that tell me I don't have to be alone.

Once my mind is right and my body is begging for her more than ever, I put her chin gently in the space between my thumb and index finger.

"Turn around."

32

Claire

I'm curled up next to Jay, my head on his chest, after what might have been the single best sex of my life. We're both still in our post-coital daze, him stroking my hair and me tracing the outline of the rose on his forearm. We have yet to have any real conversation since we finished unless deep sighs and "Wows," and "My Gods," count as full sentences.

My stomach growling atrociously breaks the silent bliss, causing Jay to spring to life.

"Oh shit, what time is it?"

Sitting up on my elbow next to him, I answer. "No idea. My phone is in my purse which is all the way out there." I point in the direction of the living room.

"Mine's in my jacket pocket. I'll be right back."

He stands and hoists up his underwear, then his jeans, but not before I catch a glimpse of his rock-solid backside. Man, that thing is what they write rap songs about.

He heads towards the kitchen where his jacket still lays sprawled out on the island. The one piece of clothing that was not tossed carelessly somewhere on my floor. I take advantage of the moment alone to throw on his white button-up that just barely covers me and slip into the bathroom.

Sitting down, I replay the experience in vivid detail, and even the memory is completely exhilarating. It was like my body was sleeping before him and was just now woken up, tingly and heavy like after you sit on your foot, and it falls asleep beneath your weight.

It was like Jay being vulnerable about his brokenness, and the way I still needed him despite it, released something inside of him that had been locked away, just clawing to get out. His ability to possess yet empower, control yet liberate, dominate yet give me reign, quite simply, turned me on. Between his commands on where to go and what to do — *"Lay back,"* *"Turn over,"* *"Look at me, Claire"* — and his physical strength and natural power, he was the director, and I, his willing participant.

The sound of him opening and closing drawers in my kitchen startles me from my trance. I wash my hands and walk out of the bathroom just as he walks back into the room. Scanning my dangerously short ensemble, he turns his lips inward, eyes now glued to the hem of the shirt.

"And I suddenly don't hate that shirt as much as I did before." He walks over to me, throwing a stack of something on my bed.

"Looked better on you," I say as he moves closer.

"Not even for a second," he argues, bringing his hands to the gap where the last button used to be before he ripped it open in my kitchen.

He moves one hand to the back of my head while he pushes open the flap of fabric now button-free at the bottom of the shirt. As he moves his lips to mine, he presses the pad of his thumb just barely to my center, and my stomach lets out a growl I'm pretty sure my neighbors could hear.

We both smile, our faces just inches apart, and the tension between us settles as he speaks.

"Anyway..." he laughs. "Good news or bad news?"

"Bad news first, always." He drops his hands and brings them to his hips.

"We missed our reservation by an hour." He walks over and picks up the papers off the bed and looking closer I see now that they are takeout menus. "Good news is, I found like six different menus for places that deliver."

"You can thank Chloe for those." I take the menus, shuffling through them. "Pretty much every time she comes over she either brings food or insists on ordering some, so I just started collecting menus." My stomach growls again. Thankfully, it didn't wake any sleeping babies this time, but it's still as embarrassing as ever.

"Let's get you fed," Jay says and my eyes shouldn't dart to his crotch, but they do because, of course, they do. He laughs and holds up two menus. One is Chinese and one is for the burger place down the street. The idea of slurping lo mein in front of Jay this early in the game has me sweating, so I tap the burger menu.

"Burger Barn it is."

He takes my order and then walks to the kitchen to make the call. I put on new underwear and the same pajama tank and shorts set he's already seen by the time he comes back.

"Twenty minutes," he says. Looking at his shirt on the bed, he drops his shoulders in disappointment.

"I thought you might want your shirt back," I say and he nods begrudgingly before sliding his arms into it. I move to him, helping him button it back up and rolling one sleeve as he does the other. My hand runs down the silhouette of the person he has tattooed on his forearm.

"Who's this?" I ask.

Emotionless he says, "Huck Finn."

"I love that book!" I gasp, still holding his arm. "We read that in my sixth-grade honors course two years ago." He forces a smile but his eyes lack expression.

"I read it a lot as a kid," he says. "Well, my brother used to read it to me at least." My face softens at the admission. Another personal piece of him he's offering to add to my collection.

"When was the last time you saw him?" He turns away picking up the discarded menus, but I see the way his body changes as he does it.

"About seventeen years."

I completely freeze, shocked by his response. He said it had been a long time since he'd seen him, but seventeen years? What I want to say is "Why?" "What happened?" "Where did he go?" but judging by the tension in his jaw, it's not a story he wants to share.

Instead, I say, "That's a really long time."

And a simple, "Mhmm" is the end of that conversation.

In my attempt to lighten the mood, I sit on the bed, leaning back on the headboard. "What about the other tattoos?"

"What about them?" he says, sitting on the side of the bed, still fiddling with the menus.

"Tell me about them." I play with a loose string on my bedspread, wondering if I should have changed subjects altogether.

"Well, we've talked about this one." He points to the naked lady that he supposedly got on the night of his twenty-first birthday because Ronan bet him a hundred bucks he wouldn't do it — he did.

"And this one." He rests his palm on the outside of one bicep, which is hidden by his shirt but that I know holds a tiger, his first tattoo at fifteen. A symbol of strength and vitality.

"And now you know about this one," he says, turning his forearm so I can see all of Huck — hat, pipe, everything.

"What about this?" I roll his wrist to reveal the inside of the same arm and a bird that sits, wings spanned from end to end.

"It's a sparrow. Ro and I each got one when I turned eighteen. They're known for their loyalty and resilience. Sparrows are extremely adaptable. They can survive in all kinds of difficult situations." He looks at the tattoo thoughtfully, like he's remembering all over again why it's there.

"Like you," I say, brushing his cheek with my thumb.

He looks up to me and leans into my touch.

"I meant what I said before, Claire." His voice is low and gravelly, his eyes despondent. "I'm—"

"Perfect." I cut him off, using the same word he used to describe me, just last night.

"Not even close," he sighs.

"Well, neither am I," I say matter-of-factly. "And that's what you said to me. Am I supposed to believe that you were lying when you said it just because I don't think it's true?"

His eyes bounce back and forth between mine, taken aback by my response.

"I'm serious." I turn to him, his head now back, resting on the head-board. "Don't dish it out if you can't take it too."

"Claire, that's not what I—"

"I'm not done." I'm not sure what has taken over me, but this want, no *need*, to get through to him that he is more than what's happened to him, takes over. He shifts his whole body so that he's facing me head-on. "I get it. You have a past and baggage, and okay, you're not perfect, but neither am I. And I need you to stop worrying about damaging me and start accepting that I want to be here." I take his hand in mine. "That I'm *choosing* to be here." He sits up straighter, rubbing his thumb up and down each of my knuckles.

"I'm choosing you, Jay. All of you. Even the parts I don't know yet. Because I *want* to know them. I *want* you. And I *need* you to believe me."

In one swift movement, he picks me up and lays me on the bed, his tall frame casting a shadow over top of me.

"What are you doing?" I say weakly, suddenly searching for breath.

"Believing you." It's not exactly what I meant, but I struggle to argue as he plants suggestive kisses on my chest.

"Was it something I said?" I ask slyly, coaxing a soft chuckle from him that's like music to my ears.

"Will you just lay still?" he growls, lifting my shirt and moving his lips further down my torso.

"The food will be here in like ten minutes!" I protest as he grips my waistband.

He looks up at me under hooded eyes, a playfulness about him that I'm seeing for the first time tonight. I'm reminded that there are so many sides to the man in front of me. To the man that I realize I'm falling for.

He winks, wiggling my shorts slowly to my knees. "Plenty of time."

33

Jamison

I wake up, reaching across to the other side of the bed, feeling for Claire but coming up empty. Rubbing my eyes, I scan her room, only to find she's not there either. I slide my jeans over my underwear and head toward the bathroom.

I swish with mouthwash I find on the sink, and check my reflection. I look surprisingly rested considering I haven't showered, and I'm in desperate need of a cigarette. I guess spending all night either talking — or not talking — to Claire, is somehow more refreshing than sleeping alone with my tormenting thoughts.

Opening the bedroom door, I'm hit by the smell of coffee and the sound of a quick *tap tap tap*. Claire, who somehow looks more beautiful in the morning, is sitting on the couch with her legs crossed like a pretzel and her laptop perched on top. Her face is serious, but bright, as she stares intently at the screen.

"Good morning," I say, leaning on the door frame. She looks up at me quickly and twitches like I caught her off guard.

"Now that's the reaction I was looking for," I joke.

"No, no!" She slams her laptop shut. "Sorry! I was just kind of...in the zone."

"Oh yeah?" I say, walking towards the kitchen. "With what?"

I look back to see her crack open her screen and type out another stream of taps before shutting it again.

"It's nothing."

"Well, don't let me interrupt you." I pour myself a cup of coffee from the pot into the extra mug she left sitting on the counter, then hold it out to her.

She grabs her cup off of the coffee table and takes a sip. "No thanks! This is already my second cup."

I look at the time. It's still early. "How long have you been up?"

"Just an hour or so. Woke up feeling..." I join her on the couch just in time to see her cheeks flush pink. She looks at me side-eyed. "Inspired, I guess."

I sip my coffee, the steam, and her confession both hitting me warmly. "To write?"

She leans back against the couch. "Mhmm."

She sounds relaxed, but her stare, currently fixated on her **Is It Friday Yet?** coffee mug tells a different story. "Can you at least tell me what type of writing it is?"

She plays with the screen of her laptop, lifting it open just an inch, then lowering it shut, open-close, open-close, clearly uneasy.

"Well, it's nothing *yet*," She brings her mug to her mouth, presumably giving herself extra time to respond. Speaking into the cup before the liquid touches her lips she adds, "But eventually I hope it becomes my first novel."

My eyes grow wide, impressed, but her floodgates instantly open. She begins rambling, over-explaining the whole idea.

"I know, it's crazy. I mean I've never written anything before. Well, anything real. Like, for anyone besides myself. I just, I don't know, I've seen the impact that books can have on kids, and I thought maybe I could write something that might make a difference to someone someday." She takes a deep breath. "It's silly."

"It's not," I say almost instantly. Her gaze, which avoided me throughout her whole explanation, snaps to mine.

"It's not?"

I twist my forearm so my childhood hero is on full display. "It's not."

She finally relaxes into the cushions, a soft smile spreading slowly across her mouth.

"I read a lot growing up," I say. "Still do actually. Books can help you escape, you know?"

"I do," she says tilting her head curiously. She squints her eyes like she wants to ask a question, but I lean over and press a kiss to her temple, leaving the conversation there.

"So, what's your plan for the day?" I ask.

"I have to go to my parent's tonight. We do dinner every Thursday."

"It's Sunday," I say dryly. She smiles and carefree Claire is back.

"Correct, but they're going away for the Fourth of July weekend, and this was the only night they could do it. Dad has to work late to get ahead before they leave and mom has a bake sale and karaoke fundraiser this week or something."

"Wait, at the same time?" I ask.

"What?"

"The bake sale and karaoke. Is it at the same time?" I know these church groups get crazy, but the thought of someone singing off-key with a mouth full of muffin seems a little too wild, even for them.

"Oh, no, two separate nights."

"Ahh. Makes way more sense." She places her laptop and mug on the table, shifting her legs to the side.

"So, anyway, dinner tonight," she repeats.

I nod in understanding but in reality, I can't relate at all. Weekly dinners with your parents? Just *dinner* with your parents? What's that like? I try to look unbothered, but my expression must betray me.

"I'm sorry," Claire says, putting her hand on my knee. "I didn't mean to babble on about my mom and dad. That must be hard to hear."

Out of nowhere I'm annoyed at myself that she feels like she has to take care of my feelings. "It's fine, Claire. I don't just fall apart whenever someone talks about their parents. You have them. I don't. The end." I shut it down quickly, the subject and the lack of nicotine leaving me suddenly unsettled but she doesn't take the hint.

"So, they aren't around at all?"

It's a fair question, considering I'm not one for details. Still, it's not something I really feel like talking about, now or ever, but especially now as I feel myself growing restless. I shift in my seat trying to get comfortable until I realize it's not the couch making me uneasy. I need a goddamn cigarette.

"I never knew my dad." I lead with the easiest of the two, figuring the best way to get past this conversation is through it. Talking about an actual stranger is way easier than talking about someone who became one.

My dad was one link in the chain of losers that dragged my mom down. From what Jackson told me when I asked, he found out she was pregnant with me and split the next day. Bred from a real fucking winner.

"I saw a picture of him once — on the obituary I found in my mom's bedside drawer. She sent me in for a lighter and I left with the only information I ever learned about my father." I take a sudden interest in the last bit of coffee that swirls in my mug, channeling my agitation elsewhere.

After a silent moment passes, Claire clears her throat. "And your mom?" It comes out practically a whisper.

I finish the last sip and stand to refill it and to avoid sitting still. "She died. Three years ago." I walk towards the kitchen, my back to her. "I hadn't seen her for a while. And she wasn't really around before that." I sound casual like I'm telling her the weather, but inside, the blood in my veins begins to bubble.

"What about the pineapple pizza story?" she says dimly from the couch.

I should be touched that she remembers, but at the same time that she speaks, my blood boils over. I hit the heels of my hands on the granite and whip my head around to her, "I was like four when that happened, Claire."

I wince as I turn away from her again, hearing the harshness in my tone. There's a moment where she doesn't respond, and I panic thinking of all the ways I'm already fucking this up. Walking away, snapping at her — why would she stick around when a simple conversation leads to something like this?

"And what about after that?" Her voice is thick, and I hate that I'm the reason. I speak the next words reluctantly, my voice still gruff, the weight of each word heavy in my chest.

"I was in and out of foster homes for nine years, Claire. Nine. There was no *after that.*" I reach for the handle of the coffee pot, like a lifeline. Anything to focus on besides my confession.

Before I make contact, Claire's arms are wrapping around my bare waist, her head resting on my back, her breath causing goosebumps on my skin. She squeezes me like the pressure of her arms can push all of my broken pieces back together.
And maybe they can.

I instantly relax, the temperature of my insides cooling from her touch alone. I cross my own arms over hers before turning without breaking her embrace. Only now that I've moved, do I feel the dampness where her cheeks once brushed against my spine. A wave of guilt washes over me as I realize my biggest fear — I'm afraid that my brokenness will end up breaking her too.

I rest my chin on top of her head. "Fuck, Claire, I'm sorry."

She lifts her chin and I pull back to see her face. Her brow is creased, but her amber eyes are cloudy, tears streaking her perfectly pink cheeks.

"You have nothing to be sorry about." She searches my face like she's looking for visual understanding. My throat constricts and my jaw tightens, my body's reaction to the lump that is forcing its way up my chest. If only she knew how wrong she was.

34

Claire

When I get to my parents, my dad is on the phone outside, pacing in the driveway.

"I'll take a look at everything and be in touch."

With my windows down I hear him end the conversation. He blows through his lips and drops his phone in his shirt pocket as I turn off the engine.

"Hey, Claire Bear." He meets me at my door and kisses me on the top of my head.

"Hi, Dad."

"Car's looking like it could use a wash there, isn't it?"

Scanning the car I see a few dirty patches and one spot on the corner of my windshield where a bird used my glass as an outhouse. Could it use a wash? Sure. Is it worth pointing out? Only to Dad.

"Maybe," I say, closing the car door. "Who was that you were on the phone with?"

Dad cracks his neck to the right before answering. "A guy who is interested in buying the Maverick." By his tone, you would think that *the Maverick* is the name of his first-born daughter rather than a car he intentionally listed for sale.

"Low dowry?"

"What?" he asks, confused.

"Never mind." I link my arm through his and direct us toward the door. "So what's the problem?"

"I don't know, Claire. He's not from around here so most of the conversation and negotiation has been through calls or emails. It feels a little..." he searches for the word. "Disconnected. And I'm not sure I'm quite comfortable with that. I told him I'd look over his offer and get back to him."

I stop on the front steps knowing he won't speak freely if he thinks what he is about to say will worry Mom.

"Dad, do you think maybe you're having a hard time finding someone you're okay with buying the car because it's your final tie to Grandpa?"

He considers this, chewing on his bottom lip. "You know, Claire, maybe you're right. Good or bad, your grandpa was my father and despite sometimes feeling less than, I loved him dearly. As a parent, I understand now that you don't get everything right. Maybe part of me wants to hold onto what's left of him, even if it's something he got wrong."

I nod understanding that my own parents aren't perfect, but knowing I'll miss even their flaws and imperfections when they're gone.

"You know," Dad unhooks his arm from mine and puts it around my shoulder. Giving it a slight squeeze he continues, "You're wise beyond your years, Claire Bear."

"Oh, I know," I say, giving him a teasing smile, then reaching for the door.

He whispers as he pushes past me, going in first. "Must have gotten *that* from your dad."

"Oh, Claire, I saw Margie at Bag Bingo on Tuesday!" Just the name Margie makes me flinch. Mom doesn't notice as she sips her sweet tea. "She said she saw you at Whisk!" A slow whirlpool of nerves begins forming in my stomach.

"Who were the blondies for, honey?" She looks at me with a closed-mouth smile, blinking slowly.

"Oh, just a friend." I look at my plate to avoid drawing attention to my lying eyes.

"Hmm…" I can tell she's contemplating whether or not she should push the issue and the whirlpool current quickens. Thankfully, she pivots. "She also told me that your picture is no longer on the Jefferson website. You should really contact HR about that."

Damn you, Margie. I should have known all of this would get back to Mom. If you thought gossip was bad in high school, you should meet the women of my mother's church. Honestly, I can't believe it took a full twenty-four hours for her to spill the tea. I play with the potatoes on my plate, buying time to think of what excuse I should use now.

I know at twenty-four I shouldn't be this worried about telling my parents that I lost my job. I just know how they're going to react. Dad is going to get all factual — "What about bills?" "Have you found a new job?" "You know you can't just let your degree go to waste." And Mom is going to get emotional and cliché — "Oh the poor kids!" "What will they do without you?" "When one door closes, another one opens." "Just pray about it, Claire."

I'm just not ready for the hysteria. And I'm especially not ready to tell them that I'm not really all that upset about it anyway.

I decide it's now or never. The anxiety of telling them is bigger than the anxiety about the actual situation, and I just want it out in the open.

"I don't think contacting HR is really going to change much," I say, hoping they take the hint.

"Well now, Claire, that's their job, honey. Clearly, someone's made a mistake."

"There was no mistake, Mom."

Now Dad chimes in. "Well if they took you off the faculty page, honey, there clearly was."

I'm really going to have to spell it out for them. Time to just spit it out.

"I'm not going back to Jefferson next year."

Mom looks at Dad curiously. "I don't understand."

This is just painful at this point.

"They cut my position, Mom."

They both look at me with confused expressions.

For. The love. Of God.

"They fired me! Let me go. There is no need for me. I'm done. Finished. Hasta la vista, Jefferson." I only finish because I have successfully run the gamut of ways to tell them I am no longer employed.

By the look on my parents' faces, you would have thought I told them I was moving to England, marrying into a British gang family, and planning to help smuggle stolen guns across the border.

"It'll be okay, guys."

"Well what about money?" says Dad.

"And the children?" says Mom.

"Have you been looking for a new job?"

"Yes, a new job! You know what they say — when one door closes just look for a window!"

"You spent a lot of time and money on your schooling, Claire Bear, it'd be a shame for it to go to waste."

"Well, we'll just have to add this to our prayer list, now won't we, Thomas?"

Okay, wow. I was spot on.

I wait to see if they're done, my neck cramping from the tennis match that I just witnessed. When the silence tells me they actually want a response, I express everything I'm feeling.

"My principal wrote me a great recommendation. I have been keeping my eyes on the job postings, but honestly, I'm not sure I want to go back into the classroom."

My dad goes to speak, but I continue before he gets the chance.

"Please, Dad, just let me finish. I know how much you guys invested in me becoming a teacher. I know because I invested a lot too. Maybe more in some ways. But over the last few years, I've realized that despite being good at it, I don't love what I do. My lesson plans lack enthusiasm,

I'm not excited about going to work, and I'm feeling really burnt out when it comes to everything that goes with it. The constant emails and conferences, parent complaints, and student pushback didn't bother me so much when I felt really connected to what I was doing, but now, it's just exhausting.

And I don't know what my plan is. I'm hoping that I have that figured out by the end of summer, but right now, I feel really good about forging a new path for myself. Maybe not something that is completely out of the realm of education, but I'm pretty set on leaving the classroom behind."

My parents look at each other, then back at me, but no one says a word.

"I know you're probably disappointed in me. You're probably worried about a million things, but all I can say is I'm sorry and I promise that despite what you may think, I have really thought this through." I stab a green bean with my fork and use it to push the others like a snow plow.

It's all out there. Well, besides what I would actually like to do, which is begin writing my novel. But all of the details that are set in stone have been said and despite getting a great jump start this morning, it is way too early to even mention that I really want to write a book.

I'm startled when my mom reaches across the table and grabs my hand. My green bean shovel halts consequently. I look up to find tears in her eyes. Great, this is way worse than I expected. Biting my lower lip I look down again.

"Claire Elizabeth Dawson," this can't be good, "If you think that we could ever be disappointed in you for following your heart." She turns to Dad. "Well, then we failed you somewhere along the way."

My eyes shoot to hers as she blinks away a tear. Dad touches her arm but looks not quite in my direction. I am shocked, no, astounded. I told them I was done teaching and the world didn't stop. No wars have started. Hell, even the dinner plates are still fully intact. It never even crossed my fanatical mind that they wouldn't be upset, let alone that they may even support me.

Where the nerves once swirled, now sits a massive brick of guilt. I was so quick to assume that my parents, Dad especially, would be critical of my choices, that I didn't even stop to think that maybe they would understand.

"Thank you, guys," is all I can manage underneath all of this emotion.

Mom clears our plates, quick to leave the room and "gather herself" as she would say, calling out, "I'll get dessert" only once she's in the kitchen.

I play with my napkin, unsure of what to say to Dad now that I've exhausted all of my energy on just telling them the truth.

"Thanks again, Dad," I say.

"For what?" He looks at me almost expressionless.

"For understanding I guess. And supporting me."

"Understanding, sure. You're my daughter, Claire Bear. Nothing would ever stop me from loving you." I smile proudly because I know he's right. My dad may find fault in the little things, but there has never been a question in my mind of whether or not he loves me anyway — a luxury I'm now seeing not everyone has.

An image of Jay hunched over the counter pops into my mind and my smile flattens. I'm not sure we're at *love* just yet, but I plan on making it my mission to show him what it means to be cared for. To make sure he never feels that sting with me.

"I know, Dad."

"But I never said I supported this."

I rip the napkin I'm playing with in two. "What?"

"You're throwing away everything you've worked for. And why? Because it's not *fun*?"

I stop him. "It's more than that."

"Right. You aren't thrilled to go to work every day. I hate to break it to you, Claire, but most people don't jump out of bed to run to their jobs in the morning."

"Dad, I'm twenty-four—"

He cuts me off. "Correct. You are twenty-four years old, Claire." He stands, his chair skidding against the hardwood floor, then walks around the table to where I still sit, dumbfounded. "It's time to grow up, kiddo." Kissing me on the head, he leaves for the kitchen.

I hear the water running and dishes clanking as my parents clean up dinner, completely unaware that I sit behind the wall, the rug ripped right out from underneath me. I'm frustrated and angry and I'm not even sure if it's at him or at myself for not seeing this coming. I know Dad, and just as he said, he'll love me through this, but to openly not support me?

I can see it now. Not much will change except for maybe receiving emails with job listings for classroom teachers with subjects like **Just Think About It** or **Something to Consider**. He won't be openly mad or throw a fit, but he'll sneak in reminders anytime work comes up or passively bring up the fact that I am unemployed.

I didn't expect a *Just Fired!* lawn sign or an *Officially Unemployed* wall banner, but for once, I thought maybe he could keep his opinion on the matter to himself and just stand behind me.

Mom has her thoughts on it, I know that, but at the end of the day, if I'm happy, she's happy. By tomorrow, she'll be on to the next meal train or craft fair. She'll be sad for me when the subject comes up, but once the dust settles, all will be well.

But Dad will never let this go, not completely. It'll be an ongoing game of Whac-A-Mole trying to dodge his subtle digs and that thought alone is enough to exhaust me already.

At this point, I'd at least take the lawn sign.

35

Jamison

I've had a little bit of pep in my step the last couple of days if I'm being completely honest. I'm trying not to get too used to it because from my experience, happiness never lasts long, but ever since Claire and I spent the night together, I can't seem to wipe this goddamn smile off of my face.

Of course, like always, there were parts when I nearly fucked it all up. Like when I let my lack of nicotine, and forgiveness, get the best of me. But even then, Claire and all of her goodness seemed to rectify it. We spent the whole night getting to know each other physically and the whole next day learning one another in every other way. Most of me is terrified — scared beyond belief to be giving this much of myself to someone, but it's like I can't control it. When I'm with her, I'm another version of myself. A version that is more relaxed, more open, and more like the person that I want to be. Like the type of person who talks about the type of person they want to be. Which is why I am here, at Sean's house, voluntarily showing up without force or a guilt trip.

I step onto Sean's porch and put out my cigarette before knocking on his teal door, amazed as always, that Sean has a *teal* door. Most of his house amazes me actually. Sean lives in the house he grew up in, which alone blows my mind. I lived in so many houses that I wouldn't even be able to tell you which one was my childhood home because they all were. Or none of them were. But Sean has lived in this one since he was a kid.

Just recently this year, his parents both retired and decided to buy an RV and travel together. I thought that only happened in movies until he told me. So, now Sean lives in a three-bedroom, two-bathroom home in a quiet development, a few streets over from my apartment. The house is light gray with a white porch railing wrapped around the front, flower boxes hanging from the windows, and a *teal* wooden door.

"It's open!" he calls from inside the house. I texted him earlier saying I was coming by since our days off happened to align. I haven't gotten a chance to catch up with him much so far this week. Holiday weeks are always jam-packed to make up for lost business, and since we're closed on the Fourth, this week is no different. Normally, I wouldn't think anything of it, but Claire has asked more than once if Sean is okay after this weekend.

I'm hit with the smell of ramen noodles first thing in the morning as I pass through the door. Sean may live in his mother's house but her home-cooked meals left when she did. Where Mrs. Bell would make hearty comfort foods like beef stew and shepherd's pie, Sean now gets by on frozen burritos and packaged noodles.

"Dude, I swear to God if you aren't wearing pants..." I yell down the hall before entering the living room. The last time I was here, Sean was three episodes deep in a Law and Order Special Victims Unit marathon, drinking soda through a Twizzler straw and not wearing pants. Is he a sixteen-year-old girl going through a break-up? No, he just relaxes like one.

"No promises!" he calls back and thankfully for him, he's kidding. He is, however, eating ramen with plastic training chopsticks with a smiling panda at the top.

"Sometimes I question how you're an actual adult," I say looking at his meal. He shovels a heap of noodles into his mouth, slurping up the ends. He chews only half before speaking.

"I'm a grownup when I have to be. And otherwise..." He gestures to his current situation. The TV loop today is Cops reruns and there's no Twizzler straw, but that panda is definitely looking at me.

"Well, grownup," I mock, "Are we going to talk about Neon Nights?"

"No." He stops me immediately, and I'm not sure if it's from embarrassment or hurt. From what Zeke has been talking about at the garage, Maddie seems to have found herself a new boyfriend in the guy she was dancing with at the club. If anyone understands not wanting to talk about the shit that bothers them, it's me, so I follow his lead and shut it down.

"Okay then, so what else is up?" He gets up and puts his bowl and chopsticks in the sink.

"Nothing really." He spins around, folds his arms, and leans on the kitchen counter. I've known Sean for a while now and at this point, I can tell something's bothering him. Unlike me, he usually does want to talk about things, so adding that into the mix, seals the deal that he knows about Maddie and it's bumming him out. I try to switch subjects to something that usually excites him — social gatherings.

"Are we still grilling for the Fourth now that your dad's not here to burn the burgers?"

The last couple of years that Sean and I have been friends, he has had a small group of people over to celebrate the Fourth of July. It's usually just the guys from the shop, Ronan and Mikey, and a couple of other stragglers, hanging out, drinking a few beers, and listening to Sean's terrible taste in music. Mr. Bell always dries out the burgers and Mrs. Bell always makes up for it in sides — potato salad, pasta salad, cornbread, and homemade mac and cheese. It's the type of celebration I don't mind — a small crowd of people I mostly know, laid-back food, and no fancy dress code.

"Sure are. I told Mikey and Ronan when I saw them at the restaurant and the guys at the shop when I was there yesterday. I invited my neighbors but they probably won't come and now I'm telling you. I guess that's pretty much it."

I want to ask if he maybe invited Maddie, but I have a feeling I already know the answer. I also want to ask if I can bring Claire, but I don't want to rub having someone to bring in his face.

"Bring Claire," Sean says before I even get the chance to ask. His voice is low but sincere. "And she can bring whoever. The more the merrier."

This guy's a class act. He's a total weirdo, but one of the nicest guys I know.

"Thanks, buddy," I reply as he stares at the floor. He pushes off the counter and saunters back to the couch. Right before he sits, he looks back at me, still only halfway in the room.

"You too, man," he says and he doesn't have to explain.

He sits on the couch and turns the volume up on the TV. I glance around the room before heading toward the couch. It's only when I look back at where I'm coming from, that I see it. Sitting right on the edge of the counter closest to the doorframe is a small black box still wrapped neatly in a purple bow.

It hits me then just how lucky I am. You have a guy like me — a complete wreck, a shitty past, and not a pot to piss in. And then you have a guy like Sean — capable of both growing up and letting loose, a loving family, a stable home, and fucking Twizzler straws and panda chopsticks. One of us has someone who, for whatever reason, seems to be interested in sticking around, and one of us can't even seem to get noticed. Never in my life did I think I would be the lucky one.

I shoot a text to Claire just letting her know I'm thinking about her. This is all new to me, but I'm leaning into saying how I feel when the timing seems right. Then, I set down my phone and my pack of cigarettes and join Sean on the couch, as sirens pour from the TV.

"So, what'd this guy do?" I ask as the camera zooms in on a cop following a truck in a high-speed chase.

"Oh, this is good," Sean says sitting up. "You're never going to believe this."

36

Claire

I smile reading Jay's text, checking my phone on my way out of the tutoring center.

JAY: Hope you're having a good day.

Ever since our "date" the other night, we've hung out or at least talked every day. It's completely unexpected that Jay and I have gotten so close, especially so quickly, but it's a welcomed surprise.

"Hey, Claire!" I hear my name whisper-yelled from across the library. When I find the source, I see it's Mrs. Wilder, the mother of the fifth grader, Josie, I just tutored in English.

"Ooh, sorry, I meant Ms. Dawson." She gives an apologetic smile, looking to the Young Adult section where Josie's scanning the graphic novels.

"Claire is fine," I say.

Normally I would insist on parents calling me Ms. Dawson, for professional reasons, but being that I no longer have any of those, I don't really have a preference.

Mrs. Wilder flashes a quick grin and then continues. "I heard you're not coming back next year." She creases her brow, looking to me for something — clarification or an explanation maybe. I feel my cheeks grow warm, the topic still not comfortable, especially after dinner with my parents.

"Unfortunately, no. I'm not." I readjust my bag on my shoulder looking for something to occupy both my hands and my mind.

"That's such a shame," Mrs. Wilder states. "Josie absolutely loved your English class last year. I have never seen that girl more interested in reading than when it was a book you chose." She turns back to Josie. "And that's saying something."

My heart swells from the praise. This is why I want to write novels kids will love. Because although teaching ended up not being for me, there are so many other ways to help grow a child's world and love of reading.

"I'll really miss all of my students," I reply, and it's true.

"Well, they will surely miss you as well." She pats my shoulder and then calls for Josie. "We'll see you next week," she says and turns to leave. Josie attempts to wave over her shoulder while balancing a stack of books a foot high piled in her hands.

I watch them leave, the first pulse of sadness coursing through me since hearing I won't be returning to Jefferson. I've been anxious of course, nervous even about where to go from here, but until now, no part of me was truly sad to be leaving the classroom.

It was only when Mrs. Wilder assured me that my students, the ones who it is all about, will feel my absence, did I realize that part of me is sad to see some of it go. Not necessarily the planning and the grading or the emails and meetings, but I'll miss the students who looked forward to my class, who bought into my lessons, and who were eager to learn. I'll miss the ones like Josie.

I spy the vending machine on my way to the exit and I'm suddenly hit with the overwhelming need for brown sugar stuffed in a crumbly puffed pastry — an emotional support PopTart. I grab a dollar bill from my wallet and flatten it against the side of the machine. I'm on my third attempt at getting the thing to take my money when two strong hands come from behind me and slide into the front pockets of my shorts.

I know from the smell alone that it's Jay, besides the fact that I can see his reflection in the glass. Just for fun, I say the first name that comes to mind.

"Oh, Mark, I'm so glad you're here." I rest my head back onto his chest at the same time that I question why Mark's name was the first to appear in my mind. Jay pulls me closer to him, his hands still in my pocket. Leaning over me, he puts his mouth dangerously close to my ear.

"Try again."

My whole body tenses at his words, and I'm now craving way more than a PopTart to ease the gloom in my chest and the heat further south.

I spin around, tearing his hands from my shorts, and make a point of putting my money back in my bag just to create some space between us. I tutor here almost every day and the last thing I need is for a parent or student to see me practically panting over this man.

"Who the hell is Mark?" Jay shoves his now free hands in his own pockets and leans in closer.

"Oh, you know, just one of my many prospects..." I say and Jay folds his arms across his chest. Unable to even play along with this storyline, I add, "I'm kidding. Mark is nobody." I pull a piece of my hair from his black v-neck. "And he's especially not you." Looking up at him, he smiles, his hazel eyes squinting slightly, but his arms falling to his side.

"Good," he says, pressing a gentle kiss to my temple. "I thought we could get lunch."

I look back at the vending machine, the brown sugar PopTart taunting me from behind the glass.

"Well, that's what I was trying to do," I mumble more to the PopTart than to Jay. "But lunch sounds great."

He eyes the machine behind me curiously and then nods to the door.

"This was a nice surprise." We step onto the street, the sun sitting at a perfect high noon.

I look for my car, forgetting I parked down the next block because my session fell right before story time, and therefore, there was not a spot in sight within stroller-distance of the front entrance. Luckily, that let out fifteen minutes before my session ended, and it seems Jay was able to park right in front.

"I was just leaving Sean's, and I thought I'd try to see you. I'll drive." He points to his truck, opening the door for me when we get there.

"How's Sean?" I haven't seen him since the incident, but I did see Maddie and her new man walking into Busy's on my way here.

"He says he's fine." Jay starts the engine and *Iris* plays from the radio. "I did see the present he got Maddie on the counter though so he must have snuck that off the gift table before he drank himself into oblivion the other night."

"No, not the earrings!" Jay told me about the gift and as a woman I can say, I was both shocked and impressed.

Jay nods, his lips pressed together. For someone who constantly talks about not getting attached to people or having no one in his life, he sure seems to have a soft spot for Sean and his rejection. I grab his hand that's resting on the gear shift.

Gestures like this have gotten easier, and more frequent, since this weekend. We both seem to feel less unsure about touching or showing signs of affection, me more so than him, but it does lead me to wonder what *we* are.

"So. where to?" I ask.

"I thought we'd go somewhere different," he says and leaves it at that. He turns up the radio and the Goo Goo Dolls sing out about wanting just that *one* person to know who you really are.

We pull into a parking lot about thirty minutes later. The building in front of us looks vintage. Like an old trailer covered in stainless steel panels and a green awning. The simple, bold sign reads, **P.J. Diner**.

"What is this place?" I look around, pretty sure Jay's Chevy turned into a time machine somewhere between the library and now.

He chuckles and points to the sign. "This is the best food *out* of town."

I'm a little skeptical of consuming food from here, just going off of how old the building looks, but all of that changes the second we step inside. We walk through the glass doors, a bell ringing overhead, and are hit with an oddly erotic combination of mashed potatoes and some sort of apple streusel. It's the type of place where right at the front is a window display of desserts and pastries that were made fresh that morning. Everything from Boston creme pie to sticky buns, to fruit tarts made from whatever is seasonal. The type of place where you still bring your order slip to the register to pay, and they only take cash. The type of place where single metal stools line a breakfast bar, ripped vinyl stretched over the seats left open for regulars and solo diners. That's where Jay leads me.

He gestures for me to sit on the corner stool and then takes the seat right next to it. An older woman with curly red hair and bright pink lipstick on both her mouth and her cheeks comes over to us smiling cheerfully.

"Jamison Errington," she says, placing her hands on top of Jay's that he has resting on the counter. "It's been a long time."

"Too long," Jay says. "Paula, this is Claire. Claire, this is Paula. She makes the best monkey bread pancakes I've ever had."

My mouth starts to water just thinking about whatever monkey bread pancakes are when Paula corrects him. "They are the *only* ones you've had, and I don't make them, my husband does."

"Well it's your recipe," Jay says and Paula winks in my direction.

"So, what are you doing here without Mel?" Paula questions as she wipes up the space in front of us. Immediately my heart drops into my stomach. Is Mel an ex? Did he bring me somewhere he's brought all of his other girls?

"I just thought I'd bring Claire this time." Paula smiles, but all I can think is, *will someone please tell me who Mel is?*

"Two regulars then?" Paula asks looking only at Jay.

"Please," Jay says. Then to me, he adds, "What do you want to drink?"

I stutter, still thrown off by the Mel comment. "Just a coffee," I answer. And because my mouth is suddenly the Sahara, I add, "And a water, please."

Paula nods sweetly. "You got it." She turns to the beverage station and grabs two plastic cups and a coffee mug. When she returns, she puts a mug of black coffee and a cup of water in front of me and a fizzy soda in front of Jay — root beer.

Jay opens one straw wrapper and sticks it in my water, then another for his soda.

"So, are you a regular everywhere you eat or just the places you take me?" I joke.

He chuckles as he takes a long sip of his drink.

"If you haven't noticed, I don't love being social. So, I go places where the people know me and act accordingly. No one here or at Enzo's is going to try to small-talk me to death while I eat my meal. Plus, I know the routine — the menu, the parking situation..." He looks at me sideways, smirking around his straw. "You know, no surprises."

I reach for cream and sugar for my coffee as I try to sound nonchalant.

"So was Mel part of your diner routine?" I avoid looking at him because I know how it sounds. He spins his stool so his feet rest on the bottom of mine.

"Mel was a part of my *life* routine. She was my case manager while I was in foster care." I look up and see he's biting at his bottom lip. "Every time I moved houses, she would bring me here first. Her way of softening the blow I guess. It became our...twisted tradition you could say."

"Oh, Jay, I'm sorry, I didn't mean to—"

"It's fine, Claire." He puts his hand on my knee. "I like that you ask questions. That you care." He brushes his thumb back and forth and goosebumps shoot up my leg.

"I do," I say almost too quickly. "Care." My eyes shift from him to the counter. "Just so you know." He inhales deeply, staring off to the side.

After a few seconds that feel like hours, he finally looks back at me. My eyes meet his and it's like he's piercing into my soul like he has so many times before.

"Me too, Claire." He holds my gaze, only breaking it when Paula returns holding two large plates.

"Jack says you better not leave without stopping back to see him first."

She puts one plate in front of each of us with three fluffy pancakes covered in ooey-gooey cinnamon goodness, powdered sugar, and banana slices. Next to the pancakes is a cup of syrup, a pad of butter, and a pile of...french fries?

I look at Jay who is already cutting into the pancakes.

"Just trust me," he says.

And I do.

A terrifying amount I do.

37

Jamison

Claire pulls up right as I stomp out my cigarette, but not before almost passing me first. I wanted to grab her on the way to Sean's house, but she remembered how close I live to him and insisted that it made no sense for me to drive to her apartment first. I tried to convince her that the extra ten minutes really didn't matter much to me, especially if it meant she didn't have any excuse to finally see my place, but that girl is scary persistent.

"Hey, no fair! That's cheating!" she calls out the window, her body reaching across the middle console toward the passenger side.

"I have no idea what you're talking about," I say despite knowing *exactly* what she's talking about.

"I told you I'd pick you up at your place, not in front of Enzo's! I was heading around back and almost passed you completely."

Okay, so she's persistent, but I am nothing if not resourceful. Technically I agreed to her picking me up at my apartment. Technically my apartment is inside Enzo's, which I am currently standing in front of. She grunts and roughly one percent of me feels slightly guilty for manipulating her like this, but the other ninety-nine percent is completely satisfied seeing the fucking adorable pout now plastered across her face.

I walk to the window, my elbows resting half inside. "Technically this *is* my place." Her pout grows more prominent as she hunches back into her seat.

"You know what I mean." She juts out her bottom lip and the way I instantly want to suck the thing off makes my stomach tighten.

"You're adorable," I say without realizing and it's only by luck that she thinks I'm still teasing her. "And I'm sorry. Next time, okay?"

"Promise?"

"Pinky." I stick my arm through the window and hold my pinky out to her. She looks at me sideways and then back at the steering wheel like she's deciding whether or not to forgive me for my grievance.

"Fine." Her pinky finds mine. "But next time you let me be a gentle-man!" Our fingers embrace and I remember the last time I did something so juvenile, so innocent.

"You'll find me?" I stand in the doorway, Ronan on the porch, his duffle bag carelessly thrown over his shoulder. His case manager Marcus is waiting at the car on the street, holding the passenger door open.

Ronan moves in a step closer, his voice hushed like what we are saying is only for us. "I said I would, didn't I?" He did, but honestly that never really means much to me, coming from him or anyone else.

The last two weeks, having Ronan as an ally has been so different for me. But despite that, like everyone always does, he is leaving, and as much as I want it to be different, I know better than to get my hopes up.

"I will, Jay." He pushes his bag up higher on his shoulder and holds up his pinky. "I swear."

I laugh at the babyish gesture, but the look he gives me is dead serious.

I hook my pinky around his and he spits over his shoulder. I have no idea what the loogie is for, but I follow him blindly, doing the same.

Six days later, the house phone rings while I should be in sixth-period history. There is only one person who would call when they know everyone else is supposed to be out of the house.

I run to the phone from my bedroom, skipping steps two at a time from the second floor.

"Hello?" I pant hesitantly, my voice low and breathy, my body suddenly flooded with the anticipation I promised I wouldn't have.

"I said I would, didn't I?"

I can hear music from the backyard as we walk around to the back of Sean's house. Biggie is telling his hunnies that he loves being called Big Poppa as we push open the gate. Sean's playlist ranges from classic rap and hip hop to hillbilly country music, each song always aggressive in its own way and never appropriate for the time that it's played.

"Biggie, Sean, really? It's the Fourth of July and like two in the afternoon." I put down the assortment of cheeses, crackers, nuts, and fruits that Claire called something French and the six-pack that was my contribution.

"What? Haven't you guys ever seen *Hardball*? What's more American than baseball?" he calls back. We all scoff.

"Your soundtrack is always spot on, buddy!" Mikey yells. He comes over and claps me on the back, then hugs Claire. "Welcome to Hell," he whispers to her before they end their embrace.

"Is it really that bad?" She asks back.

Ronan, who followed Mikey over, replies, "Oh, it's bad." He turns to me. "Remember when you said he tried playing *Margaritaville* at Rick's party last year?"

"Well that doesn't sound so bad," Claire says.

"It was to celebrate his fifth year," Mikey adds.

"Sober," I finish. Claire closes her eyes and smirks like she's embarrassed *for* him.

"Or how about when he woke us all up the morning after your twenty-first by blaring *Beat It* on full volume," Mikey says.

"Oh my God." I shiver at the memory. "We're hungover as fuck and all I hear is Michael Jackson."

Claire chuckles. "Better than Curtis Jackson," she says and after half a beat, all of the guys burst out laughing...except for Sean. His eyes shift between us like a pinball, which only makes us laugh even harder. Claire, who is making that puppy dog face at him like she did after Neon Nights, explains the joke.

"That's 50 Cent's real name."

Sean cocks his head to the side, his eyebrow creased. "Huh," he says. "No shit." And the laughing starts all over again.

It's nice to see Claire interact with the people I'm closest to so easily. Ronan and Mikey, and I guess more recently Sean, are the closest things I have to brothers anymore, so bringing her around when we do things is like my fucked up way of introducing her to family.

I grab the two of us beers from the shared cooler and we spend the next fifteen minutes bouncing around to some of the guys from the shop, and a few of Sean's neighbors who decided to stop by. When we've made our rounds and we (Claire) have sufficiently made small talk with each individual, we replenish our drinks and find shade under one of two giant trees in Sean's backyard.

"Thank you," I say. "For coming." I hold out my beer bottle and she clinks hers to mine.

"Thank you for inviting me."

"Ehh, technically Sean invited you." I shrug one shoulder, and wink at her while sipping my beer. Her hair is back in a tight ponytail today and the undisrupted view of her face shows off her features in a whole new light.

"Is that so? Well, it's good to know *someone* wanted me here."

She teases a smile, but despite the lightness of the situation, my body stills. I have the same feeling I had when I first told her I liked her. Like the words have been slowly chipping away at a wall I once built and they've finally busted through to the other side.

"I wanted you here," I say evenly. She slowly lowers the beer she was sipping and looks at me intensely. I step to her, suddenly sweating through my shirt, yet still unable to control my words.

"I want you everywhere I am, Claire. And I want to be wherever *you* are."

200

"Me too." She breathes heavily. "All the time."

I pull her to me, dropping a kiss behind her ear. Her head lolls back and she pulls me closer.

"Jay," she whispers.

I feel myself growing harder between us and I know there are a dozen other people here, but it's like we're in our own bubble, floating and weightless.

I run the tip of my nose to the base of her shoulder and she trembles beneath my touch. Her hands find my waist and I exhale, my breath forming goosebumps on her skin. I'm seconds away from ditching this party when *The Real Slim Shady* pounds through the speakers. Her shoulder bucks beneath my mouth as she starts laughing hysterically.

Moment gone.

Bubble burst

Sean and his fucking timing.

38

Claire

As if this day could get any better, Chloe finally shows up several beers and lawn games later. I wouldn't say I'm drunk, but between the combination of my buzz mixed with the excitement that she's here, I all but tackle her to the ground when she walks through the gate.

"Woah," she says, steadying us both. "Down, killer."

"Where have you been?" I ask. After watching Jay and Sean get crushed by Ronan and Mikey for the third time in a row at Cornhole, I decided to call in reinforcements.

"Okay, first, you texted me like a half hour ago, hence why I look like this." She gestures down her outfit — gym shorts, sneakers, and her tight, strappy, yoga tank that says **Spiritual Gangsta**. "And B. I had to stop for snacks." She holds up a family-size bag of potato chips and a box of donuts.

"Nothing says "Happy Birthday, America" like fried food and processed sugar," Jay says, coming up behind me. He drapes an arm across my back, his hand landing in the back pocket of my shorts.

"Well, hello to you too, Jaymes," Chloe says.

"Not my name."

"Whatever, Jayson. Listen..." She shoves the food into his one free hand, the chips just barely balancing on the box. "Where's the bathroom because I came right from the studio and nama-pee-my-pants if I don't find one soon."

"I'll show you," Ronan chimes in from the grill. He hands the tongs to Mikey and beelines it right for Chloe. I don't know Ronan all that well, but I can't help but notice the way Chloe's steady resolve wavers for just an instant when Ronan places his hand on her lower back, guiding her toward the house.

Jay kisses my temple before heading to dump Chloe's snacks onto the food table. I take the opportunity to pull my phone from my purse that's been hanging on the back of a chair since I texted Chloe.

I'm surprised to see three missed calls from Dad, one from Mom, and a missed text from each of them. Instantly, panic overtakes me. My throat grows tight and there's an itchy heat that threatens to engulf me completely in flames. I immediately think the worst. They crashed their car on the way to the hotel, they're broken down on the side of the road, someone is sick, someone is hurt. I fumble my phone attempting to open my messages. Dad's is first.

DAD: Call me.

Typical. And in no way helpful being that "Call me" from Dad could mean "Just wanted to say hi" or "My whole family is dead." I let out a frustrated grunt and steady my shaking fingers to flip back to the message screen. I click on Mom's name next.

MOM: Hi, honey. Dad thinks we may have left the garage door open and the Maverick's inside. He's sort of freaking out. Could you please go over and make sure it's closed?

Relief washes over me. I type out a quick reply letting her know I'll get it done and take a cleansing breath. There's nothing like a quick panic attack to celebrate our country's birth.

Jay must see the alarm still on my face when he returns because as soon as he looks at me, his hands are on my shoulders, his face bent to meet mine.

"What's wrong?"

"Nothing," I say. "I had all of these missed calls and texts from my parents but they just need me to run to their house really quickly. It's nothing," I repeat more for myself than for him. I take another deep breath and he relaxes with me.

"I'll drive."

"No, that's okay, you don't have to leave the party. I can come right back."

"Claire," he says. "Wherever you are, remember?"

It's so simple, but it means...everything. I press a soft kiss to his lips and when I pull back his eyes stay closed. It's like I can see his layers falling to ash all around him.

When he finally opens them, he nods toward the door. "Let's go."

The panic I had just minutes ago definitely sobered me up, but it's only when I get to the car that I realize I probably shouldn't have driven anyway. Thank God Jay insisted on coming with me.

I felt bad leaving Chloe as soon as she got there, but when I went to tell her I was leaving, she and Ronan were dropping shot glasses into pints of beer. I explained the situation and her exact words were, "Sounds good, Claire. Bombs away!"

So here we are, pulling out onto the street from Sean's house to go to my parent's and for some reason, I'm still nervous.

"You okay?" Jay asks and this is the second time tonight that he's been able to read my worry.

"Yeah. Is it weird that I'm anxious about you going to my parent's house even if they aren't there?" He noticeably stiffens, his jaw and hands both tighter, the naked lady on his forearm dancing from the way he keeps flexing and releasing his fingers around the wheel. "Not because of you!" I add. "It's just, the last family dinner didn't go so great. I told them about not going back to work."

He nods in understanding, his eyes still on the road. "Tell me about them," he says.

"My parents?"

"No, the shirts Chloe's always wearing with the weird sayings on them. I just need to know what store they're from." He chances a look in my direction and the corners of his lip curl just briefly.

"Ha ha very funny," I say. "But jokes on you because she buys them online."

"Yes, your parents, Claire."

My heartbeat quickens like it's entering fight or flight, and I'm not sure if it's the fact that this is the same topic that caused tension before or if dinner the other night has now made me acutely aware of my parent's strengths and weaknesses. I've never really talked about them like this before. Being an only child, I didn't grow up having siblings to complain to or talk to about this kind of thing. There was no "Oh my God, Mom's the worst!" or "Can Dad like take a chill pill?" It was always just me, internalizing all of the good and the bad and tucking it away until well — maybe right now.

"Mom is," I pause looking for the word. "Positive. No matter what the situation, she's always upbeat. She's constantly moving, doing things for others, hanging out with her friends, and volunteering, and it's like she somehow just keeps going. Where most people's social battery would drain, hers must run off sunshine and Jesus because it never runs out.

She willingly picks up a lot of slack for my dad who works all the time and instead of buckling under the weight of two people's responsibilities, it's like she just grew extra arms to carry the load."

"She sounds great," Jay says and the tightness I feel in my chest is a mixture of gratefulness for Mom and sadness for him.

"She is."

"And your dad?"

I draw in a deep breath and Jay notices.

206

"Not so great?" He asks.

"No, no, Dad's great too. He sacrificed all of his time to work hard for us. For me. To make sure I went to the best teaching school and that my classroom had everything it could ever need."

"But..."

"But, he's very critical of things. Always quick to point out every little, or big, imperfection. My grandfather never really noticed things and Dad knows he misses a lot from work, so I think when he can, he makes it a point to notice everything."

"That sounds hard," he says.

"It was tough on him growing up."

"On you, I mean." I don't speak and I think it's because he's right. Only, who says that?

Who says it was hard growing up with a man you loved and looked up to, but who through that closeness, also made you highly aware of your flaws? Who says that to someone who grew up with no one? Luckily, we pull up to my house before I have to.

All too quickly I reach for the handle of the passenger door, any buzz that was once lingering, now completely vanished. Jay does the same on the driver's side and we both get out, pausing to look at each other over the top of the car.

"Looks good to me," Jay says, gesturing to the closed garage door.

I lift up on the handle of the rolling door and it doesn't budge. Then, I walk to the entry door next to it and jiggle that handle. Nothing.

"Okay so, false alarm I guess," I say, shrugging to Jay. "But while we're here, do you mind if we go in? I have to pee like a racehorse."

"You and Chloe with the world's smallest bladders."

"Aw, thank you."

Once inside, I throw my keys on the entryway table and head right for the hallway powder room. Jay stays behind to have a cigarette outside. While I wash my hands I think about what he said in the car.

I guess growing up with two parents who love each other, a roof over my head, and plenty of food, I always felt privileged. Like, who was I to complain about anything? But now, I see the need for perfection, the back-handed criticism of my choices, the black-and-white thinking that teaching's my path and anything else is wrong by default, isn't right. It's not a glaring issue, but it's *my* issue and it's okay to deal with it.

I walk out of the bathroom, a newfound sense of motivation, at the same time that Jay walks through the front door. He smiles without showing his teeth and I have the sudden urge to press my mouth to his closed lips.

So, I do.

"What was that for?" he asks.

"Just because."

"Well, in that case," he slips his hands around my waist and brings me to him, our bodies pressed together from chest to feet. Kissing me, he softly glides his tongue over mine and walks us backward until we collide with the entryway table. My keys fall to the floor as the vase that sits on top wobbles side to side. I quickly steady it, his lower half still pinned to mine.

"We can not have sex in my parent's house," I whisper, turning back to him.

"I'm not sure you quite know what having sex means if you think this is it," he whispers back.

I playfully push him off of me. "You know what I mean. Plus, I'm starving. Let's see if they have anything to eat." We left before the grilling was done and by the time I thought to eat the charcuterie board I brought, it had spent hours on the food table baking in the sun and was questionable at best.

I lead Jay into the kitchen, spotless except for the miscellaneous catch-all that always seems to collect on the island. A few papers, a pair of reading glasses, a notepad with just enough empty pages left in it that Mom can't quite bring herself to throw it in the trash.

"It's like the junk drawer of the entire house," Mom always says. The place where things that don't necessarily have a home end up when you're putting everything else in the place it belongs.

I go right for the fridge as Jay lands with his forearms on the island, busying himself by rifling through the papers. My parents clearly knew they were going away because every shelf in here is bare.

"Okay, there's half a loaf of bread, cheese, and like six strawberries, so I'm thinking grilled cheese." I spin around and see Jay is now standing, a furrowed brow, heavy breathing, palms pressed flat against the granite.

"What? If you don't want grilled cheese I—"

"It's not the food," he cuts me off. He rakes his hand through his hair, then brings it to the paper lying in front of him and spins it in my direction.

I drag it across the counter. It's a sales contract for the Maverick. I guess Dad finally picked a buyer. I drag my gaze back to Jay who is staring at the paper as if his eyes could ignite it into flames. I feel an instant drop in my stomach. Jay loves this car. I knew it when Sean mentioned it at Monroe's. Of course, it would be hard for him to see it go to someone else. Or maybe he was interested and never got his chance.

"Oh, Jay. I wish you would have said something, I could have talked to my dad."

"It's my brother, Claire."

"What?" I shake my head, feeling like I have whiplash from the change in direction. Jay walks around to the other side of the island where I'm standing.

"Jackson Benningfield." He points to the buyer's name at the top of the contract. "That's my brother."

"But your name—"

"Is Errington, I know. His dad stuck around for a while. I have my mom's last name."

The whiplash returns as I try to sort out what's happening. My dad is selling his car to Jay's brother? Who Jay hasn't seen for nearly two decades?

"How?" I ask because there is no way the world is this small.

"I have no idea," he says. "He was always interested in cars. Hell, if I took the time to think about it, I would have realized he's probably why I felt pulled to them too. I just...I didn't even know he lived around here."

"He doesn't," I say, remembering back to what Dad said in the driveway when he hung up the phone. Jay's eyes dart to mine, searching each one for an explanation.

"The last time I talked to my dad about the car, he said he had a buyer who was interested in the car but lived out of town. He was supposed to send his information over so Dad could look at it and decide what to do."

Jay turns the documents over, his eyes landing on the signature lines down below. Jackson's jagged scribble on the buyer line, Dad's loopy cursive on the seller's.

"Well, I guess he did," is all he says. The silence that follows is filled with questions and lost time — time that two brothers spent as strangers instead of fighting through life together.

"I'm so sorry, Jay." I bring my hand to his shoulder but he gently shrugs it off.

"Let's get out of here."

"Do you want to talk about it?"

"Now, Claire," he says. "Please." He turns and walks to the front door, the jingle of my keys telling me there's no changing his mind.

39

Jamison

This has got to be some kind of fucking joke. As if to say "Oh you thought you'd be happy," the universe throws something like this into existence.

When my brother left, that was it. No calls, no visits, nothing. I was just a kid, torn between being proud that he got out and being angry that he abandoned me to do it. As I grew older, I tried to find him, to reach out — the only person I ever looked for — but he didn't want to be found. At least not by me. And now, gone over half my life, he pops back up to buy *my* dream car from Claire's dad.

There it was, Jackson Benningfield, the name I stopped googling a decade ago when I realized I'd never see or hear from him again. His address, phone number, email, every possible way to contact him, written plain as day for a goddamn stranger.

Information apparently too good for me.

I'm strangling the steering wheel back to my apartment in absolute silence. Claire looks at me every few seconds, her flushed face full of concern, but I can't bring myself to talk to her. It's like all of the walls that she has been tearing down brick-by-brick, just rebuilt themselves out of solid cement.

This is why. This is why I don't open up to people, why I don't let them in. If they won't hurt me, I'll hurt them. I know she says she doesn't care about my past or the baggage I bring with me, but I do. I won't let my shit, and my reactions to it, break her with me.

I pull around the back of Enzo's to the empty parking lot. The sun is just starting to go down, the streetlights not quite on. Pulling into a space, I keep the car running.

"I think you should go," I say to the windshield rather than to her. There is no way that I'm adding Claire coming into my shitty apartment to tonight's list of events.

"No."

"Claire," I say sternly, turning to her.

"I'm not going anywhere."

"It's not a good time. I just...I need to figure all of this shit out."

"Then I'll come with you."

"I don't want you to come with me," I snap back.

Her head pulls back and I see her wince just briefly before sitting up straighter, face serious.

"I'm sorry," I sigh. "I'm just going to sleep on everything before I have to get up early for work tomorrow."

"What happened to believing me?" she snaps back.

My mind drifts back to that night. Where she told me she *wants* me, that she's choosing *me.* But that is exactly why I can't let her in. If I have any chance of keeping her, I need to shield her from this.

"I just can't right now." I grab the door handle and push it open in one swift motion. "Just go."

I'm halfway to the back door of my apartment when I hear the engine shut off and her car door slam. I reach for the knob but she pulls my arm back until my hand falls into hers. I look at the ground, too embarrassed by the shitshow that is my life. Claire deserves so much better than this.

"Look at me, Jay." When I don't move, she says it again, stronger than I've ever heard her speak. "Look at me."

I slowly meet her gaze and behind her glossy eyes, I don't see sadness or fear or regret. I see strength.

"Wherever you are."

I never really understood the expression, *tugging on your heartstrings.* I'd hear it in a movie or a book and wonder how anything can make you feel something so strongly. Like my "heartstrings" must just hang around limp, because I'm not quite sure I'd ever feel that connected to something. But then I met Claire, and the way that she's looking at me now feels like my strings aren't just attached to her, they're anchored there, pulling me in but at the same time, holding me steady despite the current.

"Say it again," I say, moving toward her.

"Wherever you are," she repeats.

"Again."

"Wherever you—"

My mouth collides with hers, one hand on her throat, the other in her hair. She hums and I feel the vibration beneath my palm. I tilt her head to me, sinking deeper into the kiss, as she slips her hands up the back of my shirt. We fall into a rhythm of sweeps and strokes until I reluctantly move one hand from her to the knob behind me. Pulling it open, I step backward over the threshold, our lips still connected. We walk like this, intertwined until we come to my door. I pull away from her just long enough to slide my keys from my pocket and into the lock.

Once we're inside, I pull her to the bed and she straddles my lap, her legs on either side of mine. We bite and suck and tug and grind until our bodies are entangled, a web of limbs knotted together.

I roll her to her back. My teeth graze her neck as I hover above her, and she moans into my ear. Desperate for friction, she throws both legs around my back and pulls me so my lower half is flush with hers, my weight settling between us. I'm hard, she's panting, and there's a need here that's palpable.

I for one, need her body, her heart, everything, all of it. *Wherever you are.* I feel it in my chest as sure as a second heartbeat.

Where. Ever. You. Are.

I break free from her hold and slide down to her waist. Undoing her buttons, I slide her shorts and underwear off in one strong pull. She gasps and I groan, the sight of her enough to save me alone.

I stand, stripping myself of my clothes. First my shirt, then my jeans. She mirrors me, sitting up, throwing her own shirt to the ground, a masterpiece of peaks and valleys.

"Fuck, Claire." It comes out hitched as she crawls back on the bed, and I tear off the one remaining material between my body and hers.

I climb back on top of her, kissing slowly up her calves, then her thighs, pausing at her middle just to sample her. She bucks beneath my touch.

"Jay," she whispers.

I taste her again, but it's not enough. I continue up her hip, then the curve of her side, to the space between my favorite curves. Her nails are in my hair, then on my back and I throb between us, only for her.

Where. Ever. You. Are.

"Be with me," I blurt and I'm as caught off guard as she is.

I feel an elemental shift deep in my soul. Like my insides are rearranging to make room for the parts of me that have been stored away, dust brushed off and cobwebs wiped clean. This is one of those moments that gets broken down into befores and afters. *Before* I gave my heart to Claire and *after* I risked it all.

"Be with me." It comes out more intentional this time, but still foreign in my voice.

She freezes beneath me. "Jay," she says.

"I mean it. Be with me, Claire."

She focuses on me, her amber eyes dilated.

"Shit." I hang my head, my weight balanced on my hands on either side of her beautiful face. "I'm fucking this all up."

Claire tilts my chin up, her face once again only inches from mine.

"Jay, I—"

"Will you please just fucking be with me? Please?"

"So polite," she says, after a painful amount of time, and I watch the corners of her lips turn up before the hunger returns to her eyes.

"Yes," she says.

"Yes?"

"Yes."

I push into her and the rest of the world goes quiet. My mother, the men, cornfields, alcohol, Jackson, closets, Huck, cars, Mel, bruised fists, wet cheeks.

"Just a little longer, Jamison."

"Make a life for yourself."

"Be a good boy."

All of it. Silenced.

I push into her over and over, the only sound in my head matching the rhythm of our bodies.

Where. Ever. You. Are.

40

—

Claire

I open my eyes and stretch, the twin-sized bed somehow feeling even smaller without Jay in it. I glance at my phone and see he must have left for work. I scroll through my notifications to see if there are any texts from him or Chloe, but there's just Facebook requests and email alerts.

Jay wasn't kidding. His place really is tiny, but despite its size, it feels just like him. Some parts are reserved and steady — the bare white walls or the single framed photograph of him in the middle of Ronan and Mikey, sitting on his dresser. Then, some parts are personal and warm — the sandalwood candle on his kitchen counter or the worn toothbrush next to the soap by the sink for cleaning his nails of stubborn grease. And then of course, some parts are just...Jay — the mismatched sets of dumbbells, the books and ashtray on his bedside table. All of these things together fill this small space with everything it needs — him.

Jay gave me more of himself last night than he ever has. The circumstances were completely unexpected, my dad selling the Maverick to his long-lost brother, but it's like fate pulled that whole story together for this reason. Like I had to do a favor for my Dad, not once, but twice, for me to meet Jay and get us here. Better yet — and I'm not one for "everything happens for a reason," — but if this was the endgame of losing my job, disappointing my parents, and stressing about my entire future, it just might be worth it.

I reach for my phone again and send a quick text to Jay.

ME: Text me after work. I miss you already.

I know he might not be able to check his phone for a while, but I want to remind him I'm waiting for him when he gets done. I swipe out of those messages and into my chain with Chloe to send her one too.

ME: Are you alive?

After a few minutes, and no texts back, I decide to head home. I have no idea when Jay gets done today, but I'm in desperate need of a toothbrush and a shower.

Feeling refreshed, I sit down at my computer to work on my novel. I still haven't heard from Jay or Chloe, but I have writing to do anyway. I've barely touched my draft since I started it the other day and after last night, I'm flooded with ideas. Apparently, all I have to do is have mind-blowing, heart-shattering, sex with a man who is tall, inked, and handsome, to bring my dreams and fantasies to fruition.

I had the idea to write a story about childhood best friends growing up together after Jay told me about his tattoo with Ronan. He told me sparrows survive in all kinds of difficult situations, and it made me think that friendships, or any kind of relationship, are like that too. Whether it be the type that finds each other in the thick of the heavy stuff, like Ronan and Jay's, or the type that just deals with new problems as they come, like mine and Chloe's, all relationships experience trials.

Which is why I started my story of Alice and Owen — two young friends who grow together and take on life's hardships as a team. I hope that by telling the story in two different time frames, one with them as children and one as teenagers, young adults will be able to relate to the natural ebb and flow of a relationship as people get older and evolve over time.

Friend and friend, sibling and sibling, parent and child, the goal is that there's something relatable for all types of connections.

I write for the next few hours, continuously it seems, barely stopping for even a check in spelling. Before I know it, my computer's dying, my stomach's growling, and my hands are cramped in the best possible way. I save my document, close my laptop, and check my phone, surprised to see there's still no new messages.

Jay doesn't shock me, from what I know he rarely checks his phone as it is, but even when there's time at work, his hands are usually too dirty to even risk looking. Chloe, on the other hand, surprises me.

I scroll through my contacts until I reach her name and call her. Right to voicemail. I try again thinking it was just a fluke and again her voice pops through saying, "Sorry, I *can* answer the phone right now, I just don't want to. Leave a message. Bye!" I feel the thoughts start swirling in my mind but I remind myself it's Chloe. She probably left her charger in the car again and is just too lazy to go outside.

I occupy myself with a cup of tea and another Google search for jobs. Scrolling through the short list of nearby available positions, I expand my search and one listing catches my eye. I click on the post.

Description: Freelance writer needed for pet rescue
Responsibilities:

- Writing creative descriptions of available animals

- Interviewing adopting families for website content

- Regularly updating brochures with rescue information

Requirements:

- Relevant writing and editing experience

- Open availability to meet demands of intake and events

- 3+ years of professional writing experience preferred

Okay, so I wouldn't necessarily say I'm an "animal lover." I always wanted a dog, but Dad said no one would ever be around enough to take care of it. Then at the Start of Summer Carnival, I won a goldfish, but let's just say I knew there was something I forgot when I left for camp.

Besides that, the rescue is also pretty far from here and I have zero or less years of professional writing experience, but it does get me thinking.

I never thought about piecing work together until I could figure out my next move. I have had it so ingrained into my head that there's only one right way, only one direction, that it never even crossed my mind that there might be something that allows more time in my schedule for my novel but also pays my rent.

I favorite the post and change the job search at the top from "Education" to "Freelance Writer." Dozens of jobs populate, so many of them either nearby or remote — news journalist for a local paper, interviewer for an online memoir company, food-feature writer for a restaurant chain — now that's something I could get excited about.

The possibilities seem so vast to me. As someone who's lived the last decade or so on such a narrow path, I guess black and white thinking has become a learned trait. I condemn my Dad for thinking my life's work means teaching or failure. Am upset by his thought that if I leave education, I'm not the successful child he raised me to be. But somewhere along the line, I've started to see the world the same way. I have developed the thought that if it's not teaching, it's book-writing or nothing. That I either have to give up on my dream or take it on so aggressively that I have to give up everything else. But the world is filled with so much gray. So much beautiful, glistening silver that holds opportunities I'm just now seeing for the very first time.

I close my laptop, determined to ride out this new high.

And find my best friend.

I'm pretty sure Chloe's neighbors either hate me or are eighty-year-olds with their hearing aids turned all the way off. I am pounding on Chloe's door and not one has poked their head out to see where the fire was. I didn't even knock first, just went straight to breaking down the door. Call it adrenaline but the second I got here and didn't see her car anywhere nearby, I started freaking out.

I raise my hand to whack the door one more time, but instead of the door, my fist hits bone. I yell and two other cries follow. One is Chloe's God-awful screech and the other is deeper, more guttural — low like a growl. I focus my eyes and see a half-naked Ronan hunched over, hands to his face.

"Oh my God, Ronan!" I yell.

"Claire!" Chloe yells back. "What the hell?"

"I didn't kn...What is even happening here?"

The aftermath is pure chaos, Chloe running to the freezer for ice, me running to Ronan, and Ronan stumbling back onto the chaise behind him.

"You're not supposed to be here!" Chloe says as she wraps a bag of frozen fruit into a dishtowel.

"You weren't answering your phone!"

"It's dead!"

"Well, I thought *you* were dead!"

Meanwhile, Ronan holds his nose, blood slowly creeping from his nostril, and snaps his head back and forth between the two of us.

"Not dead! Just wish I was!"

"Hungover," Ronan clarifies. I try to steady myself, pieces slowly falling into place. Ronan, Chloe in a man's t-shirt, two glasses on the kitchen table, Chloe's **Spiritual Gangsta** tank top near the bathroom on the floor.

"Wait a second. Did you two—"

"No," they both say in unison.

"Then will somebody please tell me what's going on?"

"I got drunk," Chloe says.

"Very," adds Ronan.

"Okay, I got very drunk. Ronan drove my car home for me and *allegedly* put me to bed." She winks at me waiting for his response.

Ronan looks up from under his makeshift ice pack at Chloe with a wrinkled brow. Then he turns to me.

"I walked her in and tried putting her right to bed but she insisted on me saving her *"thug tank"* from any probable vomit. So, I gave her my shirt and put her in the bathroom to change."

"My hero," Chloe says and Ronan rolls his eyes playfully, bringing the fruit back to his face.

"I didn't have a car." He looks back to Chloe. "Or a shirt. So, I fed us each a glass of water and slept on the couch. And apparently forgot to charge her phone."

"You guys realize it's the middle of the afternoon, right?" I say.

"She wouldn't let me leave."

"I woke up late and *The Goonies* was on. Nothing happens when *The Goonies* is on," Chloe says matter-of-factly.

"She was all, *'Don't ask questions, Sonny. Take a seat'.*"

"Gambino," we both say, looking at each other knowingly.

"Okay, well, you freaked me out," I say.

"I got that," Ronan says.

"Yeah, that's my bad."

"It's fine. You pack a killer punch. Jay will be proud."

I smile in the cheesiest way, thinking about him and missing him all the same.

"I'll make sure to tell him when I see him," he continues. "I was just heading out." Ronan hands the fruit to me and turns to Chloe who looks at him confused.

"I'm sorry, but I'm pretty sure it'd be frowned upon to enter the establishment in which I work and own, not covering my nipples."

"Well, that does not sound like any sort of establishment that I'm interested in," Chloe quips.

Her familiar smile tells me there's a probable chance she's more than interested in both Ronan and his business. She goes into her room to change shirts, leaving Ronan and I alone for the first time.

It may be because I'm seeing him shirtless or just that the bar fight look is working for him, but suddenly I understand Chloe's interest. Ronan is objectively a very handsome guy.

"I'm really sorry, again," I say.

"Don't be," he laughs. "Chloe's lucky to have a friend who's so...passionate."

"Hey, you wouldn't happen to have heard from Jay, would you?"

"No, my phone's dead too. Why? Is something wrong?"

I hesitate to tell him about anything with his brother. It just doesn't seem like my place to say, and as far as not hearing from him during the day, it's not something I'm necessarily worried about. I'd love to get a reply, sure, but we all know despite his schedule, he's a man of very few words.

"No, no, I just haven't heard from him yet today."

"You know how he is. I'm sure he'll call you after work."

Chloe comes back out in a neon yellow t-shirt with a chicken on it wearing sunglasses and tosses Ronan his shirt back. He throws it over his head, careful to avoid his nose which is no longer bleeding but is already starting to bruise.

"I'll see you ladies later," he says as he walks toward the door. I shoot Chloe a *follow him* look and she hurries to meet him.

"For real, thank you for last night," she says. "And this morning."

Ronan leans in just inches from her mouth and says, "It's okay, Goonies always make mistakes." Chloe's lips part, but right before he brushes them with his, he tilts his head, landing a gentle kiss on her cheek.

"Just don't make any more," he whispers into her ear.

And that was the moment that I saw my best friend fall in love. Well, not really.

But, maybe.

41

Claire

I spent the rest of the day at Chloe's, listening to her rehash what she could remember from the night before. Apparently, Ronan told her that her car-bombing was impressive — one sentence I hope he never uses in a parking garage — and she proceeded to spend the rest of the night showing off her skills.

After ordering food from the Chinese place down the street and stuffing ourselves with crab rangoon, vegetable lo mein, and orange chicken, we watched the end of *Sixteen Candles*, and I left for my tutoring session on middle school grammar.

Somewhere between comma usage and the *you have to write out words like "are" and "you" rather than using single letters* lesson, my phone buzzed in my bag on the floor. I gave Brian, or B-Rye as he prefers, a few examples to try on his own and pulled it out just long enough to see who the text was from.

Seeing Jay's name on my screen caused me to heave a huge sigh of relief. All day I told myself that he was busy, rarely checks his phone at work, or isn't one to talk much anyway, but I couldn't silence the voice in the back of my mind that kept telling me he regrets last night and he's not sticking around. I shoved my phone back into my bag and decided I could read it later. Just knowing he wasn't avoiding me was good enough.

But then I saw the text. Long after my tutoring session had ended, I still sat, staring at the screen.

JAY: Busy day. I'll call you tomorrow.

Alright, so it was something. He had the decency to at least text me back, but after last night, and the place that I *thought* we had gotten to, I expected more than essentially a day of silence. I returned the text asking if everything was okay and it went unanswered.

My first instinct was to be annoyed, but I knew what I signed up for when I decided to start falling for a man who *told* me he's not good with communication. So, instead, I channeled all of my frustration into the book.

I stayed up way too late writing three more chapters about Alice and Owen and sometime after Alice started a new school, I fell asleep with my computer in my lap.

I wake up now, to once again, no texts or calls from Jay. Sure, he didn't say he'd call in the *morning*, but at this point, it's been twenty-four hours since he asked, no told me, to be with him and then totally ignored me.

Rather than letting the anxiety fester, I decide it's time to take a much-needed run. I change out of my pajamas and into my running shorts and tank top. I grab my headphones and turn on my **Run Like You Stole Something** playlist. By the time I stretch and get to the street, the chorus of DJ Khalid's *All I Do Is Win* is playing in my ears. An appropriate anthem for the headspace I'm aiming for.

My first mile is quick and way beyond my normal pace, but it's like my body is fueled by the stress coursing through my veins. By mile two, I'm slowing down, both physically and mentally. The endorphins hit their pace as I hit mine, calming the chaos that was rising in my head.

I pass my parent's house and see they're still not home. *Good*, I think, *because I am definitely not ready to deal with that right now*. Before I know it, I'm rounding the corner of Main Street where Monroe's Motors sits at the end. Would it be absolutely ridiculous to show up to Jay's work for a third time? Sure. Is it just as crazy to run by and look for his truck in the lot? I'm going with only slightly and that's good enough for me.

I jog by the bay doors and peer inside. Without slowing down to total creep-speed, I can't see anyone who looks like Jay. Being that he's over six feet tall, has arms like a coloring book, and is somewhat massive in size, I would think he'd be hard to miss. But, while I'm here, I decide to take my run around the back street where the parking lot is before heading back toward my apartment.

Once again, I slow down, lessening my pace just enough to scan the cars. Nothing. There's not even another vehicle the same color as his, parked anywhere near the garage.

"Claire!" I nearly trip on the curb in front of me, hearing my name being called from the direction of the shop. I slow down to almost a walk and see Sean waving a hand towel in my direction.

"Hey, Sean," I call, still across the parking lot. I'm not quite sure if this is a stop and talk situation or if he's just saying hello.

"What are you doing?"

Okay, so not only are we stopping and talking, but we're stating the obvious too.

"Just my morning run," I say awkwardly, half looking for Jay and half hiding from him too.

"Ah, good for you. I could never." He points to his very young, clearly unathletic legs. "Bad knees."

"Mmm," I say half-listening, suddenly slightly nauseous from thinking about Sean's joints.

"So, where's Jay been?" He's got my full attention now.

"What do you mean? He's not at work?" I was slightly out of breath before from the exercise, but I'm breathing even heavier now.

"No, we were both supposed to be on the whole week after the cookout, but he called off yesterday and then again this morning."

Suddenly I can barely breathe at all. My legs go weak, my heart rate quickens and none of it has to do with running.

"So you talked to him?"

"Well, Zeke did. Called both days to let him know he couldn't make it in. Not like him at all, but Zeke said he sounded fine on the phone."

He called them. Jay — who I slept with, who told me he wanted to be wherever I am, who insisted that I be with him, who hasn't called or texted in over an entire day sans six words, called them. The part of my brain that worried that maybe something had happened to him, relaxes, while the other part, which was fully convinced he was ghosting me, is going off, lights and sirens.

"I, I, I got to go," I stammer and take off in the opposite direction.

"Have fun!" Sean calls out completely oblivious to the mental breakdown happening right in front of him.

"Asshole!" Chloe says over the phone. I've been walking aimlessly way past my apartment at this point and decided calling her made more sense than listening to Taio Cruz's *Break Your Heart* on my running playlist over and over.

"I don't know Chlo, maybe it's me."

"What? As in maybe *you're* the one who Magic Miked your way into *his* pants, and then abandoned *him*?"

"If anything it was more like Paul Walkered into them from Fast and Furious," I say dimly.

"Okay, fair. My point is, *you* are not the asshole," she clarifies.

"I know, but he told me over and over again that he doesn't do this kind of thing. That he's broken, and damaged, and I somehow thought none of that would matter."

"And it shouldn't."

"Yeah, but you didn't see him, Chlo. This thing with his brother really tore him up."

"Listen, I'm just saying we all have shit."

"I think his shit is a little bigger than our shit," I say.

"Ew," Chloe says. "I'm just saying, we all have things going on. No one else is disappearing and then lying about it by omission."

"I know," I say. And I do know. But that's the problem.

Besides his "people," only I know how tormented Jay seems to be about anything and everything that's happened in his past. How he holds onto his mom, his brother, foster care, like they're lifelines instead of anchors.

"I'll keep you posted."

"You better. But Claire," she says, sighing into the phone. "He's not gone yet." She ends the call, and I'm left paused in the middle of the sidewalk.

And there it is. The center of my fear. The reminder that my teaching career, my future, Dad's support, even Mark for Christ's sake, all just...ended. Giant parts of me that came crashing down after one conversation.

"There's just no need for your position."

"I cheated on you."

"I never said I supported this."

And now here's Jay, slipping away too.

A man of few words offering not even one.

After literally hours of walking, I find myself at the shopping center with Busy's and Enzo's. I have no money with me, so coffee is out, but maybe I can at least bum some air conditioning from Ronan and Mikey.

I open the door to the restaurant, the smell of the pizza oven just coming to life, wafting toward me. Ronan, who is sitting at the register counting bills, looks at me from behind the counter and pulls his hands to his bruised face.

"Please don't hit me again," he jokes before lowering his barricade.

"Very funny," I say. "Glad to see your nipples are completely out of view."

He shoves the rest of the money into the register and comes around the side of the counter.

"What's up? Hungry?"

"Oh no, I don't even have any money. I was just wandering and was kind of hoping to cool off before heading home."

Ronan looks me up and down and takes in my sweaty...everything. "Take a seat," he says.

I find the nearest table, the one that Jay and I happened to sit at the first time we ate together and push my phone and headphones off to the side. Minutes later, Ronan comes over with a large cup of ice water and a slice of Hawaiian pizza and places it in front of me before sitting in the other chair.

"Jay told me it's your favorite." He gestures to the pizza, and I play with the edge of the paper plate.

"Have you talked to him yet?" I ask. He turns his head away, staring at the floor, thinking.

"Now that you mention it, no I haven't. Not since the cookout the other day." I nod my head and continue playing with the plate. "What happened?" he asks.

I shake my head, keeping it down, trying to hide the fact that I feel tears forming behind my eyes. When I don't speak, Ronan repeats himself. "Claire. What happened?"

I look up and the concern on Ronan's face breaks the dam. Tears fall and he reaches for napkins, giving me time to get myself together. My heart breaks for Jay, and for myself, as I tell him about everything from his brother buying Dad's car, to him asking me to be with him, to his radio silence.

Ronan drags a hand down his face before speaking. "This has nothing to do with you, Claire."

"It sure feels like it does. *My* dad's car, *our* night together, ignoring *me*."

"I get that," he says. "But Jay has been through some shit that not even I can understand."

I nod, looking back down at my untouched food.

"Did he ever tell you how we met?" he asks, and I look up to meet his sorrowful gaze.

"Mhmm."

"Did he tell you how I came into the system?"

I shake my head, no.

"My birth parents died. Car accident. A drunk driver hit them head on and they both died on impact."

My hand shoots to my mouth, my eyes watering for a second time.

"I didn't have any living relatives," he continues. "Both of my parents were only children, and my grandparents were all gone before I was even born."

"I'm so sorry," I say.

"It's okay," he says. "Yeah, there was some shitty stuff that happened there for a few years. I got dealt a bad hand and was in a dark place for a while, but after I met Mikey and my adoptive parents, things started falling back into place. At the end of the day, I get to leave this world knowing I had two sets of parents who loved me. Which is a whole set more than most people." He smiles but it's fleeting. "But that's twice as much as Jay."

I look at him and see a man who once had his life ripped apart and sewn back together. Who was once thrown in the thick of tragedy, but is now so loved and so successful. He's an absolute anomaly. But he's also absolutely right.

"Did he ever tell you his story?" he asks.

I sniffle. "Just pieces. I know about his mom being an alcoholic and the men who were abusive. I know his brother left when he was young and that he was in the system for a really long time."

He bobs his head, but his eyes wander like he's looking for something. "Did he tell you how?"

"How what?" I ask.

"How *he* got put into foster care in the first place?"

I search my messy mind for that detail but fall short. "No, he never told me that."

He inhales a deep breath, exhaling slowly before he says, "He made the call."

I look at him blankly. "I don't understand."

"He called the cops, Claire. His mom went on a bender for three days. Three fucking days she left him...alone. No food, no supervision. He was nine-years-old." He pauses, shaking his head in anger. "Jay would walk himself to and from school and on the third day, he walked himself home at lunch so he didn't have to lie about not having food, again, and he saw his mother lying in the driveway. Bruised, beaten, covered in her own vomit. Someone just left her there. Three days of drinking and drugs and some guy dumps her off for her nine-year-old to pick up the fucking pieces."

Tears stream down my face, my heart physically aching inside my chest, as I hang on to every word Ronan says.

"Jay ran inside and he knew. He knew what this would do. His mom always told him what would happen if the cops ever came, but he didn't have a choice. It was call or let his mom die right there on the street." He pauses, his nostrils flaring in rage for his best friend. "So he did. He called. The cops came, an ambulance, everything. And when Jay tried to lie, to say that this had never happened before, that she was only gone a few hours, they knew. Everyone knew. They took him that day and he spent the next forty-eight hours sleeping at the station until Mel came to pick him up."

I stare at him completely destroyed and utterly dumbfounded. This. This is why Jay carries all of this so heavily inside of him. The weight of it all. All of the guilt that he must feel, drags him down every day because he blames himself.

"But it wasn't his fault," I say.

Ronan chuffs, "Well, I know that and you know that, but try telling that to someone who was repeatedly beaten down — never knew his father, neglected by his mother, always too much or not enough for foster families. Just passed around from one house to another until that one decided they were done with him too. And now, his brother, who also left him, shows back up right when he thinks something good is finally happening in his life. Right when he finds you, Claire."

I'm suddenly so overwhelmed. By the story, Jay's past, my own feelings. By the fact that Ronan thinks that *I'm* the good. I want to find Jay, hold onto him, and never let him go. Tell him over and over that I'm not leaving. *Wherever you are*, I think. I'm not going to wake up one day and just decide that I'm done, that he's not enough. He'll never be *too much* for me.

"Did she ever come for him?" I ask, picturing my own mother who does everything for everyone. For me.

"Once. She visited him. Told him she was going to work on herself and do better. That she'd get him back when she was able to give him the care he deserved."

"And did she?"

"Not even another phone call."

I think of all the times my mom has called to check in on me. All of the *"Call me when you get there"* texts when I went out with friends or the *"Get home safely"* messages when I went back to school after a weekend home. And then I think of Jay. Waiting by a phone that never rang. For a mother who never came back.

"I have to go," I blurt, wiping my tear-stained cheeks with the back of my hand. The feelings inside of me threaten to take me down completely if I don't get out of here. I grab my things off of the table as Ronan stands, frazzled by my sudden exit. I'm halfway out the door when he calls out to me.

"Claire!" I turn to him, already bringing my headphones to my ears. "Just be there for him," he says. "It's always worked for me."

I walk out the door before he has the chance to see me come undone once again.

I run all the way home, playlist on full blast, tears still leaking from my eyes. I knew when I met him that Jay had demons. It is written all over his beautiful face, but I never knew the depth to which he carried those demons with him. Now, when I picture that face, I see a little boy, mistreated, deserted, a casualty to the system. The face of a nine-year-old who spent the rest of his life thinking he drove away the one person who was supposed to love him unconditionally.

The face sitting on the front step of my apartment building, sweating in the heat of the afternoon sun.

42

Jamison

"I'm sorry," is the first thing I say to Claire after thirty-six hours of silence. It's not enough, but it's all I can manage when I see her run toward her building, her hair tossed on top of her head, face wet, shirt clinging to her body slick from sweat — beautiful.

I've been sitting here for an hour. It's the first place I came when I got home. I ran through the rest of my cigarettes in the first fifteen minutes, trying to calm the mixture of emotions threatening to choke me from the inside out. I have no idea what else I'm going to say. I've tried a hundred times to plan it out, but nothing does her any justice. She stops just short of me, hands hanging by her side, breath heavy.

"I'm sorry," I repeat.

"You left."

"I know."

"Disappeared."

"I went to find my brother." She steps closer to me, leaning forward, then quickly pulls back crossing her arms over her chest like for just a second, curiosity beat out the emotions inside her.

"I remembered the address I saw on the paperwork at your parent's house. Turns out he's been just a few hours from Maple Grove this whole time." I chew my bottom lip as I stare at the concrete in front of her.

Finding Jackson was not a quick decision. Sometimes you know in your gut the choice you're going to make about something before you even make it consciously, but this wasn't like that. All night with Claire I laid awake going back and forth between whether or not I wanted to reopen that wound. I laid there, Claire's head on my chest, her leg thrown across me, and thought *this could be enough.*

But as much as I wanted it to be, as much as I wanted her to fill every void in my life, I couldn't let her take on those burdens. If anyone understands that one person can't fix another, can't take away the hurt and pain or the addictions of someone else, it's me. So I needed to attempt to fill this one myself.

My mother is gone. That guilt and shame have made their home and will occupy that space inside of me forever. But Jackson isn't. And when I found that out, a door cracked open that I thought was locked forever and I had to decide if I was slamming it shut or ripping it off the hinges. I tried to shake it all off ever since seeing his name yesterday on that damn piece of paper. Tried to push it out of my mind. To downplay the fact that my brother who I haven't seen for seventeen years is alive and well and buying a damn 1974 orange Ford Maverick. But I couldn't.

"What happened?"

"Well," I gather my thoughts. "First I sat in my car down the street for like twenty minutes trying to decide if I should just fucking turn back around. But then Jackson came out of the house to get in his car, and I knew if he left, I may never get my chance.

So, I just walked up to him. I told him he may not remember me, but he did, Claire. He knew without me even saying anything. He came up to me and he hugged me. He hugged me so goddamn tight like he had been waiting seventeen years to do it. He said he tried to come back for me. He came a year after he left but I was already gone. Mom wasn't home and no one knew where I was except for that I was living with a new family." I inhale deeply before daring to take another step towards her. She doesn't back away but she doesn't meet me either.

"He said he hoped that being with a new family meant that I was finally happy. Finally free." She swallows and I see her tough exterior waver ever so slightly. She uncrosses one arm, using it to pull the other in tighter.

"I told him about my life and he apologized for not doing more. We talked about where we are now and when I left," I continue, "We exchanged numbers and addresses and made plans to check in and see each other. To talk. To never let time like this go by again."

"And how did you feel about all that?"

"I felt," I pause to think. "I felt...relieved. I felt pissed — at my mom, at him, at the fucking universe, at myself. But mostly I felt so...happy."

She nods. "And now?"

"And now," I say, closing what's left of the gap between us. "Now, I feel...just so damn sorry." I put my hands on her shoulders, leaning forward so my eyes meet hers. She pulls back gently but holds her gaze, her eyes glossy with tears.

"You just left, Jay. You could have told me what you were doing. I would have understood. I would have gone with you!" Her volume rises as she speaks, but not out of rage. Out of something closer to hurt.

"No, I couldn't have, Claire, *because* you would have gone with me. I can't drag you into all of my shit!"

She shakes her head. "You're not dragging me if I come with you willingly!" At this point we're both yelling, back and forth — a tug of war.

I take a deep breath and steady my voice. "I am not going to ask you to save me, Claire."

"Why can't you ever just let me all the way in?" she sighs, stepping past me towards the building. As she pushes the door open, she turns back to me, a look of defeat written all over her face. "Maybe you should go."

She walks down the hall toward her apartment, and I follow her. She gets to her door and pushes the key into the lock.

"That's not what I'm saying," I say calmly as I catch up behind her. She turns to me and if frustration had a face it would be Claire's.

She huffs, throwing her arms in the air. "Then what *are* you saying?"

"I'm saying, I fucking love you!"

Her hands slowly fall to her sides as she stares at me, eyes wide, lips parted. "What?"

"I love you, Claire," I say softly, moving closer. "So goddamn much. And because I love you, I won't ask you to save me."

She stands motionless for what feels like an eternity then slowly rises onto her tiptoes, holding onto my forearms for support. When she finally speaks, her voice is almost a whisper.

"Then don't," she says. I focus on her, holding my breath. "Just ask me to be with you while you learn to save yourself." Her eyes shift between mine before she lowers herself back down.

I drop my forehead to hers and close my eyes relishing in what she just said. "And you will?" I ask.

"I will," she says, placing a soft kiss on my cheek. "Because I love you, too."

Claire and I walk into Enzo's not at all surprised to see Chloe leaning against the display window. From what she filled me in on, something is brewing between these two but neither of us has any idea what it is. Honestly, I'm not sure *they* even have any idea. It could work out perfectly though if Claire's best friend starts dating my best friend. It would sure make going out more a million times easier.

Claire also filled me in on her talk with Ro. It's not necessarily how I wanted her to put the final puzzle pieces together, her crying to him because I hurt her when I left, but I'm glad that he told her everything.

That day is forever ingrained in my mind. The weather outside, the sight of it all, the sound of the voice on the other end of the phone, and until yesterday, it ate me alive. It felt like I had willingly given over my mom, my family, and my entire life, to the system. Like I personally caused the next fifteen years to unfold if not from my actions then from some sort of cosmic karma. But after talking with Jackson and then

Claire, and really hearing what they both had to say, I might not feel one hundred percent better, but I'm on my way.

Besides filling me in on the time between when he left and now, Jackson and I talked all day about the years he was around. He told me stories I don't even remember. Times when I would beg Mom to stay, not to go to the bars or to leave with a guy, and she would tell me I was too young to be worrying about her. The irony there is proof alone at how lost she really was.

It's funny because I used to think about Mom coming back. About her finally calling and telling me she'd gotten better. That she had her life together and was ready for me to come home so we could be a family. *Then*, I knew I'd run to her ten times over if that ever happened. Now, I know it never would have.

Mom was sicker than any nine-year-old was capable of knowing. Jackson understood because he was older. He learned about the disease in school, and even experimented with alcohol and drugs just to see for himself what our mother could possibly have loved more than her children. He knew that nothing anyone did could help her if she didn't want to help herself. It's why he left when he got the chance.

But I wasn't old enough to get that and by the time I was, there was no more room for understanding in my heart. It was filled with so much humiliation and rage, so much resentment, that it was just easier to burden the blame than to hold her accountable.

I'm sure Mom dealt with her own shit. Guilt maybe or regret. I think deep down every mother would to some extent, but in most ways, I'm glad I never found out. I'm learning that people who love you don't make you question it. They don't leave you guessing at whether or not you'll be cared for today. Sometimes they falter. Sometimes they leave. Sometimes, like Jackson, they make the best decision of all their terrible options, but they say sorry, they come back, and they fix the things they broke.

"Claire!" Chloe turns around seeing us. She's all smiles until she lands on me. "Jay."

"Chloe," I say, but it isn't lost on me that she actually used my real name.

"It's fine Chlo," Claire says probably noticing too. Chloe squints at her as if trying to decide if she's telling the truth and then relaxes. She steps forward and wags her finger in my face.

"Fine. But if you ever go all *Gone Girl* again," She pokes me in the chest. "We *will* have words."

I look back to Ronan who is smiling behind the counter. "Received," I say, walking towards Ro to leave the girls to talk.

"Is it bad that she kind of scares me?" I ask him as I lean on the window.

"Me too, man. But is it worse if I kinda like it?" I laugh and we slap hands over the window. "Welcome home, buddy."

It hits me once he says it, that this is why everything feels so right. I've never even known what *home* really meant. Sure, my boys have always been here. Hell, now even my brother's back, but with my girl here too — I think I'm finally starting to understand.

43

Claire

Six Weeks Later

"**B**abe...Babe...Claire!"

I snap back to reality and realize I've been staring out of the window for the amount of time it has taken Jay to shower and fully get dressed. So, probably about six minutes.

"Sorry!" I say. "Zoned out there for a second."

"You should probably get that looked at," he jokes.

"Very funny. I was just trying to think of an ending."

"For the book?" he asks. "That was fast."

"No, it's just an outline for the second half. I have to plan how I want the ending to be so I can backtrack when I write the rest." He comes up from behind me and drapes both arms around my neck. I bring my hands to his colorful skin and kiss the spot where the thorn sits on the rose.

"Well, make it a good one," he says. "Happy."

I turn my face up toward his. "I will," I say and he kisses me like he has so many times in the last few months.

After everything happened with his brother, Jay and I spent almost every night together, and all of his days off. He was here so much that I joked he should just move in, and before I knew it, he pretty much had. He still has his place in Enzo's, but his toothbrush, his razor, those damn work boots, are here. And I wouldn't have it any other way.

"Seriously though, we have to get going. Dinner with your parents is in like twenty minutes."

"Okay, okay," I say. "I'm ready."

I had a few more solo weekly dinners before Jay first came along. It gave Mom, Dad, and I, the time we needed beforehand to sort everything out.

Seeing Jay muster up the courage to go talk to his brother who he hadn't seen in over half of his life, sort of made my nerves to talk to my own loving parents seem just a little bit unreasonable. So, I went over the week after that first trip Jay took and sat them both down.

I told them that I appreciated that they invested so much into me and that they put so much at stake for my education, but that their feelings about my future were not my responsibility. That my responsibility was to make sure that I don't wake up every day and wish for a life that I could just as easily make for myself.

I thanked Mom for sacrificing everything for everyone else. I told her that I was glad that she was happy volunteering and helping other people, but that my hope for her was that she would slow down and make some time for herself. Maybe follow her own dream.

I told Dad that I understood the pressure that he was under to provide for his family. I told him I understood that the lack of attention he got from Grandpa was probably really hard on him, but that he didn't need to fixate on everything I do for me to feel his love.

Both of them seemed to at least hear what I was saying. The comments and the nitpicking stopped with time, and I decided I was ready for them to meet Jay. My parents took to him surprisingly well considering a tall, tattooed, mechanic was probably not who they pictured for me. His brother even joined once when he came to pick up the Maverick. He and Jay spent most of that dinner cruising around in the car, but Jackson promised he'd bring it around next month when he comes to stay for longer.

As the weeks went on, everything seemed to be falling together. Even Dad came around to the whole writing idea, asking if he could be the first to read my novel when it was finished. I think it helps that last week, I told them about my plan once summer ends.

I decided that I'm going to spend a lot of my free time writing the book, but that I'll continue tutoring and may even pick up a few freelance jobs. Margie of all people, spoke at a school board meeting about the lack of variety in writing courses offered at the school, which her grandson Ben is apparently very gifted in. She suggested that "Ms. Dawson" return to lead a creative writing club every week after school. I got an email three days later from Principal Andrews asking if I would be interested in leading the club for a small stipend. I took the offer and just found out that it's every Wednesday starting the first week of school.

Jay was, of course, supportive of whatever I decided to do. He's reminded me constantly that a lot can go wrong in life, but anything that makes you happy just isn't one of them. So, I decided I was going to be happy. And I learned that it doesn't take much to make that happen.

"Claire, let's go!" Jay calls from the kitchen.

I decide on the fate of Alice and Owen and slam my laptop shut. "Coming!"

I grab my phone and keys off the island realizing Jay is already halfway out the door.

"Shit!" I yell. "I forgot the—"

"Already got 'em," he says, pulling his arm back inside, revealing a white cardboard box with *Whisk!* stamped on top. "Stopped on my way home from work."

I walk over to him, placing my hands on either side of his cheeks. "Home," I say and kiss him hard, my forehead settling on his. "I like the sound of that."

Epilogue
Jamison – One Year Later

"Can you grab the big serving tray off the shelf in the garage?" Claire asks, taking mini egg tart things off of the pan she just pulled from the oven.

"Sure," I say quickly, shoving a third piece of nicotine gum into my mouth. Does it count as being "better for you" if you stress chew an entire row? I switched to the gum a few months ago but days like today definitely make me miss the real thing.

Claire puts down the tray and walks to me without taking her eyes off mine. "Hey, you okay? It's just our friends and family, remember?"

"No, no, it's not that." Of course, I still have an occasional moment where the idea of socializing sends a chill up my spine, but at this point, I think it's the same as anyone who just generally dislikes most people. "Just tired. Jackson and I got in late last night," I say. She nods and lifts the side of my shirt, exposing my ribs and fresh tattoo.

"It looks so good," she says, running her finger around the outline of the Maverick that my brother and I both got permanently placed on our bodies last night. At this point, it's so much more than a car. To us it's the reason we were brought back together after way too much time apart. To me, it's the reason I met Claire.

"Thanks, babe."

"Hey, is Mel going to be able to make it?

"I don't think so, but she told me she's dying to meet you. Maybe we can get together another time soon."

"Ooh, over monkey bread pancakes?" she begs.

I kiss her on the side of the head. "Whatever you want." She smiles and then puts on her *back-to-work* face.

"Perfect," she says. "But right now...I want the serving tray."

"Yes, ma'am," I say, walking towards the door.

The garage is detached so I have to walk through the backyard to get to it. The perfect excuse to put some distance between Claire and me and get these nerves under control.

We moved in a few months ago. It was the biggest thing either of us has ever done. For me it was finally having a place that's mine. It was proving to myself that I can make a life for myself and for Claire and help us start our future. Not only that, but it was a physical structure to put meaning to the word *home* — something that, for most of my life, never even existed. And I would have never made it here without her. Or Sean.

Claire and I lived together in her apartment for a while until it was time to invest in something bigger. It just so happens that at the same time, Sean's parents decided to sell their house in Maple Grove and stay on the road permanently — with Sean's blessing of course. He always said it was too much house for him anyway. Instead, he moved to a spacious two-bedroom apartment downtown and when his parents were ready to sell, he suggested that they bypass the grueling market and give it to his favorite couple to rent-to-buy.

So, now Claire and I live in that quiet neighborhood, a few streets from Enzo's. We have a light gray house with a white porch around the front, flower boxes, and a teal wooden door.
And Sean has officially paid his debt to me.

He had one last Fourth of July cookout here and then passed the keys to us. It's now been a few weeks and we're pretty much settled in, so we (Claire), figured it was time for a little housewarming party.

I still can't believe I get to call this place home with the most amazing person I have ever met. If you would have told me over a year ago that I would be inviting all of my favorite people to a party for the home I share with Claire, I would have told you to kick fucking rocks. But here I am, and it's the perfect excuse to gather all of the people that we love without ruining the surprise.

I get to the garage and I stop to take it in, like I always do. It's small and unorganized for now, but it's the perfect size for a car I hope to one day have in here. When we were looking at the house, it was actually Claire who suggested it. I always left the repairing I do at Monroe's and thought one day I'd just buy a hotrod that was ready for the road, but she reminded me that I'm good at putting things back together that were once not at their best. I did it for myself and now, I hope to one day rebuild something that has been tossed aside and make it something special.

I scan the shelves for the plate that Claire needs and eventually find it with the other miscellaneous items that don't yet have a place inside. I grab it and head back to the house, but not before also grabbing the little white box in the back of the first drawer of my tool chest.

I open it and take a deep breath looking at the ring inside for the millionth time. When I asked Claire's parents for their permission to marry her, her dad had a million questions of course, all of which I was prepared for, but her mom simply left the table. At first, I was concerned. Is she that upset that her daughter may spend the rest of her life with me? But that changed when she came back with this. A solid gold band with a ribbon of small diamonds swirled around one large one in the center — Claire's grandmother's ring.

I had never seen something so nice, so expensive. I had never seen a family heirloom before. But where my family was the type to pass on only generational trauma, Claire's family is the type to pass on these types of meaningful and beautiful things. The type of family I will soon be a part of officially.

Or at least I hope so.

I tuck the ring box in my sock under my jeans and take the plate inside. Stepping through the back door and looking into the living space and kitchen, I look around and see Zeke talking with Claire's parents, and Sean and Rick goofing around with the other guys from the shop. I see

Ronan and Mikey checking out Jackson's new tattoo. And then I see Claire.

Her hair is down in soft waves around her perfect face, her freckles on full display from the summer sun. Her cheeks are flushed from the warmth of the oven as she dances around Chloe to pull out another tray. She throws her head back to laugh, her sundress swaying from the movement, and I'm *still* completely mesmerized by her.

"Jay!" she calls when she sees me and I'm instantly nervous like she can suddenly see inside my sock. "Just put that here. I have a surprise for you." I relax just slightly. Here I thought surprises were my thing today.

"Jay Bird," Chloe says when she sees me.

"Chloe," I say back. She wraps one arm around my waist and hugs me from the side as Claire leaves the kitchen. I do the same and lean my head against the top of hers in an embrace. Chloe and I have gotten much closer this past year. She has a tough exterior, but she's total mush on the inside — much like some other people I know.

Claire comes in from the front porch with a large cardboard box. I take it from her and put it on the counter.

"I just got a text that they came," she says shakily and I assume it's from the weight of the box until I realize what's inside.

"Oh, no shit!" I say loudly. They both slap me from either side of my body.

"Shh!" Chloe whispers.

"I didn't want to make a big deal about it," Claire says.

"Make a big deal about what?" Sean yells from the living room, grabbing the attention of all the other guests. So much for being discreet.

"Oh, it's nothing," Claire calls back, but at this point, all of our family and friends have gathered around the perimeter of the kitchen to see the mystery inside the box.

"It's okay," I whisper into Claire's ear. "This is everyone who loves you. Now's the perfect time." And I'm not sure if I'm saying it more to her or to myself.

She nods back at me and grabs scissors from the kitchen drawer. Sliding the blade down the middle, she opens the box and pauses.

Chloe, who is absolutely too short to see inside, just squeals with pure excitement for her friend. I grab Claire's hand below the counter and give it a quick squeeze to let her know I'm there.

Wherever you are, I think.

Claire takes a deep breath in and pulls out a book with a blue and yellow cover that reads, "The Adventures of Alice and Owen." She exhales, rubbing her thumb along the bottom text: **Claire Dawson.**

"Wait what's that?" Sean calls out.

"A book you dumbass," Mikey says.

"Whose book?" Ronan asks.

"Claire's!" Chloe yells at him, before trying to hide her smile.

"It's here!" Claire's mom squeals.

"Hey, did you hear my daughter's an author?" Mr. Dawson says to Zeke.

"You did it," I whisper just to Claire. She leans back into me and brings the book to her chest.

"Thanks to you," she says.

I wrap my arms around her from behind and rest my chin on top of her head.

"No way, baby, this was all you."

I feel her head move back and forth beneath me as she holds the book out again. She opens it and turns to the very first page with words. I read them over her shoulder.

"Dedication -
To all of those who were once so beautifully broken. Thank you for showing the rest of us how to piece ourselves back together."

I let out a quick gasp and squeeze her tighter. This girl who turned my world upside down in the best possible way, who brought me back to life, who saved me despite constantly reminding me that I saved myself, is thanking people like *me* for helping someone like *her.*

"I love you," I whisper in her ear.

"I love you, too," she says back, nuzzling into the crook of my neck. It's now that I realize *this* is the perfect time. I clear my throat and stand up straighter.

"Actually, there's one more box," I say.

Claire pushes off of me and looks toward the front door. "No," she says, sorting through the books on the counter. "I just ordered a handful. This was the only one."

I drop to one knee, and she spins around when she hears gasps from guests behind her. When she does, her hand flies to her mouth as her honey-colored eyes land on me, box in my hand, arm extended.

"Jay," she says tentatively as Chloe squeezes her arm at her side.

"Claire."

"What are you doing?"

"When I met you, I was just barely living. But from the second I laid eyes on you through that tinted window, everything changed. You saw the best in me when I could only ever see my worst. You broke down walls, peeled back layers — you saved me, Claire."

"You saved yourself," she whispers.

"Thanks to you," I say smiling, mimicking her from earlier. "But this life we've built, these people behind me, I wouldn't have any of this without you. My past is so messed up, but my future, with you in it, is everything I have ever wanted." I set the ring box on the floor and take both of her hands in mine. "Claire Elizabeth Dawson, I love you so much. So fucking mu—"

"Jamison..." Claire's mom calls from behind.

"Sorry, Mrs. Dawson," I say finding her in the crowd. "So much," I continue, turning back to Claire. "Will you please spend the rest of your life with me?"

Claire nods with tears streaming down her face as Chloe jumps beside her.

"I'm gonna need you to say it, Claire."

"Yes!" she says. "Of course, yes!" I drop her hands, grab the box off the floor, and kiss her with everything I have, entangling our limbs in the sweet scent of vanilla. I slide the ring onto her finger, a perfect fit, and feel a hand clap my shoulder from behind. The rest of our guests swarm Claire, but Ronan is there for me, arms open, as he always was.

"You better be ready to be my co-best man," I say, hugging him tightly.

"Wait, for real?" he says. "You swear?"

"I swear." I hold out my pinky and he smiles, wrapping his in mine, both of us spitting right on the kitchen floor.

"Ew, you guys are disgusting!" Chloe squeals, the two of us laughing hysterically at each other. "Claire, you're so lucky your maid of honor will be there to save you from these clowns."

Ronan raises his eyebrows toward me then throws a wink in Chloe's direction who tries her best, but fails, to hide her blushing cheeks. After a year, I still have no idea what is going on there. And neither do they.

"Now it's a party!" Mikey yells from the living room as Sean tinkers with the speaker we have sitting on the coffee table. I look at Claire, who is holding her hand out to her mom, smiling from ear to ear.

When I used to think about my life, I thought of abuse and neglect, pain and suffering. I was sad and depressed and so incredibly broken. Now, looking around this house, *our* house, I see my life, and it is nothing short of perfect. There's love and meaning, peace and happiness. I have my friends, my brother, my new family, and Claire — everything I could ever need.

Jackson intercepts me on my way to Claire and hugs me like a brother does. "I'm proud of you," he says and I feel it light up all of the darkest parts of me.

"Thanks, man," I say, choking back feelings.

He steps to the side and says, "Now, go get your fiancé."

I nod at him and then I do. And for once Sean's song choice is spot on as Tracy Chapman's *Fast Car* fills the room.

Beautifully Broken
The Playlist

1. Under the Bridge - Red Hot Chili Peppers

2. My Humps - The Black Eyed Peas

3. Leaving on a Jet Plane - John Denver

4. Oops!...I Did It Again – Britney Spears

5. Stairway to Heaven - Led Zeppelin

6. Crazy Train - Ozzy Osbourne

7. Tiny Dancer - Elton John

8. Raise Your Glass - Pink!

9. Rude Boy - Rihanna

10. Run Rudolph Run - Chuck Berry (Zeke's Favorite)

11. Wild Ones - Flo Rida Ft. Sia

12. Right Here Waiting - Richard Marx

13. Cat Daddy - The Rej3ctz

14. Iris - Goo Goo Dolls

15. Big Poppa - The Notorious B.I.G.

16. Margaritaville - Jimmy Buffet

17. Beat It - Michael Jackson

18. The Real Slim Shady - Eminem

19. All I Do is Win - DJ Khalid

20. Break Your Heart - Taio Cruz

21. Fast Car - Tracy Chapman

The End

Acknowledgements

Thank you to everyone who helped to make this dream a reality.

To my little girls, thank you for your patience with me and for your unconditional love. It is because of you that I strive to be the best version of myself, which most recently has included crossing *Write a Book* off of my bucket list.

To my husband, thank you for your unwavering support and encouragement. Your constant reminder to invest in myself is what got me here. Also, thank you for allowing my book to be the first you've maybe ever read willingly.

To my mom, thank you for being my rock, for always being my first call, and for lighting up when I told you about this story. Your reaction alone was everything.

To my friends that were with me along the way, you know you are more like family than anything. Every text, every "like," every time you read my manuscript, I was reminded that I have built-in fans already.

Lastly, to my dad, thank you for your strength and for showing me that life's story is a series of chapters, each one important, but none alone, capable of defining who you are. Twenty-eight years with you by my side will never be enough.